I0676378

Snowfall at Ember Lodge

A Midwinter Novel

Haven Saunders

MaHanna Media LLC

Chapter 1

The last stretch of road to Midwinter, Montana, wound like a ribbon between trees heavy with snow. Lila Moore kept her hands at ten and two, breathing with the windshield wipers. Inhale on the swish. Exhale on the clack.

She had not checked her phone in three hours.

She hadn't planned it that way.

The last thing she'd seen before turning the screen face down on the passenger seat was a subject line she recognized and didn't open. Her name sat in it, spelled correctly, which somehow made it worse.

She told herself she'd read it later, when she had distance. When the world felt quieter than it had in weeks.

The road narrowed, snow pressing close on either side, and the GPS began to falter. Lila didn't reach for the phone when the screen dimmed. She let it go dark.

Whatever waited for her there could wait a little longer.

The GPS on the dash of her rental SUV spun in circles before giving up and showing a gray field that might as well have been the moon. She didn't reroute or try again. She let it fail. Being unreachable wasn't an accident. It was the plan.

"You wanted remote," she said to herself. "You got it."

The forest opened to a wide view of water smoothed to slate. A line of mountains rose beyond it. Their tops rose into the sky like peaks of meringue. The snow had the kind of hush that made sound feel like intrusion. Even the engine seemed to quiet when she turned onto the gravel drive next to a wooden sign that read *Ember Lodge* in carved letters. Beneath the sign, a small metal lantern clinked in the passing breeze. The wind tugged sharper than it had a mile back, carrying the promise of weather closing in.

The lodge sat on a rise above the lake. A pitched snow-covered roof topped a long spine of dark logs and river stone. Two stories of paned windows reflected the pale morning, and smoke lifted from a wide chimney in a slow, steady line. The lodge looked like the kind of place artists drew on cards.

She parked before checking her phone. No signal. Not a flicker. Not even the hint of one bar.

"Perfect," she whispered flatly.

Wanting space was one thing. Having it forced on her was another.

Cold bit her cheeks when she opened the door. The air smelled like pine. Snowflakes dusted the sleeves of her black coat and caught in her chestnut hair. She tilted her head back and let the flakes fall on her face. Without thinking, she opened her mouth and tasted the snow. Though the act was childish, she couldn't stop herself from smiling. She felt free in a way she hadn't in months.

The main reason she'd chosen this place was because it was new. It was a break from her usual routine. Cold slowed things down. Weather erased timelines.

Inside, she took a moment to absorb the lobby of the old structure. Warmth closed around her immediately. The space opened in two directions. To the left, a stone fireplace big enough to stand in. To the right, a wall of windows that looked toward the lake. Chairs in worn leather huddled near low tables. A worn navy and tan wool rug spread over pine floors. A copper kettle sat on a trivet near the hearth. She felt the place settle into her bones, as if a piece of herself had been waiting here, patient and quiet. Whatever she'd been carrying couldn't quite get past the threshold.

The woman behind the desk stopped short when she saw Lila, her smile catching before it fully formed. She had silver hair pinned in a soft knot and eyes the color of strong tea. For a brief moment, something like surprise crossed her face. Then concern.

"Oh, you made it," she said quickly. "You didn't get my message, did you?"

The words landed harder than they should have.

A cold, irrational thought flashed through Lila's mind before she could stop it: *She knows.*

The instinct to turn around, to mumble an apology and retreat back into the snow, rose fast and sharp.

Lila blinked. "Message?"

"We tried to call this morning," the woman said.

Something tightened low in Lila's chest. Recognition. Or the threat of it. The kind that came before bad news. "I haven't had a signal since somewhere outside of Billings."

A man appeared from the hallway behind the older woman, tall and a little stooped, with a scarf looped twice around his neck. "No matter. You're here now. Walter Mercer," he said easily. "Owner, bellhop, and teller of tall tales when the nights run long."

The woman turned back to Lila, her expression gentler now, though the concern hadn't quite left her eyes. "I'm Ruth Mercer. Welcome to Ember Lodge, dear."

"Lila Moore," she responded with a smile. Her name had never felt heavier. Like something she was still deciding whether to carry or set down.

Walter stepped closer, resting a hand on the edge of the desk. "The weather changed faster than expected," he said, tone calm, reassuring. "Storm's swinging low. They've been adjusting the forecast all morning. We were hoping to reach you before you got too far off the main path."

Relief loosened something in her chest, slow and cautious. The concern wasn't about *her*. Not yet.

A flicker of panic stirred behind Lila's ribs, sharp and unwelcome. The timing still felt uncomfortably precise. "Should I not have come?"

"No," Ruth said at once, a hand already lifting as if to steady the moment. "No, you're fine. Truly. We're more than prepared." She smiled again, this time with intention. "However, your stay might run a little longer than you'd intended. It's up to Old Man Winter, now."

Walter nodded. "We've weathered worse. If the power goes, we have lanterns and a generator."

Ruth reached for the smaller of Lila's bags despite her protest. The foyer's heat rolled out, carrying the scent of coffee and something baking. "Come in before you turn into a snowman."

"So. The storm is going to get bad?" Lila tried to keep her voice light. *Bad enough to make leaving impossible?* she thought.

Walter set her suitcase beside the long wooden desk. "We'll keep an eye on things. You're safe here."

Safe. The word landed, welcome and heavy all at once. She hadn't realized how badly she wanted someone else to say it.

Ruth slid a leather-bound ledger across the counter. "We keep the old book for luck, even though everything goes into the computer after. Sign here, Lila Moore."

A familiar pang followed the sound of her name. Online, it belonged to subscribers, clients, and affiliate links. Here, the letters looked simple on paper and a little shaky, as if she had not signed anything in a long time.

Ruth watched her with kindness. "Coffee until noon. Then tea. Your room's on the second floor in the north wing. There's a lake view. If the storm likes us, you'll see it march across the water."

"And if it doesn't," Walter added, leaning an elbow on the counter, "you won't miss a thing. It's stubborn that way."

A soft nudge against Lila's leg made her look down. A gray cat with tufted ears and a white chin sat at her boot, assessing her like a small judge.

"That's Juniper," Ruth said. "She thinks she owns the place, and we pay rent in treats and ear scratches."

Lila crouched and offered her fingers. Juniper sniffed once, then butted her head decisively into Lila's palm. Lila stroked the soft fur behind her ears. "I'll try not to offend," she murmured. Though she wasn't sure that was as easy as it should be.

Juniper hopped onto the counter and yawned, as if bored by the idea of effort.

The front door opened on a gust of colder air. A man stepped inside and closed it firmly behind him, then stamped snow from his boots on the mat. He wore a dark beanie pulled low and a work jacket brushed with white. There was something in his posture that suggested he had learned, over time, to take up less space than he had.

"Generator's ready," he said to Walter, voice even. "Fuel line's clean. I'll check the gutters before the temperature drops."

"This is Evan Drake," Walter said, "our resident miracle worker. Evan, this is Lila. She is visiting from warmer parts for a little quiet and grounding."

Evan's eyes were a cool brown, almost amber near the center. He nodded, not unfriendly, but measuring. Not dismissive, either. As if he were taking stock instead of passing judgment. "I thought guests were holding off on arrivals until this storm passes."

"I didn't get the message," Lila said, not quite defensively, though something in his tone made her feel examined, as if she were being weighed for risk rather than welcomed. She'd had enough of people assuming things about her.

"Unfortunately, you'll find your cell phone signal is missing more than found in these parts," Ruth offered with cheerful innocence.

Lila felt the smallest flare of panic behind her ribs, hot and shameful.

A week. That was all she'd promised herself. A week to breathe, to regroup, to decide what she was going to do about the email she still hadn't answered.

The lack of signal turned waiting into something sharper.

The promise had sounded brave when it was theoretical. Standing here, with no signal and a storm closing the valley, it felt hasty.

"We keep an old landline behind the desk in case of emergencies."

Lila breathed. In. Out. The room smelled like coffee and cinnamon and wool that had been near smoke.

Evan moved closer to the hearth. He crouched and opened the iron grate, then used a poker to shift a log. Flame flared and took, then relaxed. He shut the grate without a scrape and turned to Ruth. "They updated the forecast. Storm's due by two now," he said. "We'll want the lanterns out and the extra quilts up from the laundry. I'll bring in more wood for the fire."

Lila watched without meaning to. The efficiency of the movement. The quiet confidence. Something in her chest eased.

She had definitely timed her arrival badly. Or exactly right. She turned to Ruth with wide eyes. "How much snow are we supposed to get?"

Ruth clucked softly. "Don't you worry. We'll be snug as can be. This kind of forecast is nothing new here. Walter and I will show you to your room."

The stairs rose wide and worn, the banister polished smooth by decades of hands. At the landing, a framed photograph hung slightly askew. A line of people sat along the beach with their backs to the camera, shoulders close. A few brave swimmers cut through the glacial water, arms flashing white.

Lila paused.

People who knew one another caught in the same moment. Not posed. Together because they were.

Something tightened behind her sternum, sharp enough to make her look away.

Ruth opened a door at the end of the hall. "We call this the Lake Room. It isn't original, the poet in me regrets to say, but it's accurate. The view is the point."

The room was simple and deliberate. A bed with a carved headboard. A writing desk near the window. A wool blanket folded at the foot. Outside, the lake lay dark and patient beneath the mountains as snow ticked softly at the glass. A white mug waited on a coaster next to an individual sized coffee maker. A book rested on the nightstand, spine turned out. *Essays on Living Slowly.*

"It's perfect," Lila said.

Walter set her suitcase on a wooden stand and pretended not to notice the frayed handle. "Heat works by way of old radiators. If they don't warm up fast enough, give them a swift kick in the tuchus."

Ruth smiled at the radiator. "Ignore him. If it rattles, I'll come up with a wrench, and everything will be right again." She hesitated, then added gently, "Will you be okay if we're snowed in for a few days?"

The question slipped under Lila's ribs before she could brace for it. She laughed, but the sound caught near the end. "I'll manage."

It was the same thing she'd told herself when she closed her laptop. When she decided to take a break. When she stopped reading after the first line of messages she couldn't unsee.

Ruth seemed to accept the answer at face value. "Good. Supper's at six. We don't stand on ceremony, but we do appreciate showing up on time so the soup doesn't get cold."

When they left, the quiet leaned in close, pressing into the room.

Lila unpacked carefully, lining her shirts in the wardrobe, smoothing each fold. The small order soothed her. In her other life, she organized chaos for a living. Content folders. Posts scheduled weeks in advance. Words polished until they said nothing dangerous. Until they couldn't be used against her.

Here, she placed a sweater on a shelf, and no one watched.

She set her notebook on the desk and opened it. The first page held a single sentence, written months ago in a hand she barely recognized. *I want to hear my own thoughts again.*

The urge to take her phone from her pocket and check for a signal pulled hard. Habit, not hope. She closed her eyes and breathed until it eased. There was no signal. Not here. Not with the weather sealing the valley closed.

Outside, the wind picked up, shaking the window. A chill rolled through her as the storm marched closer. Without the warmth of her winter coat, her long-sleeved cotton shirt wasn't going to keep her warm.

Lila pulled on a cardigan and went back downstairs. She told herself it was for tea. Or to sit and work on one of the puzzles she'd spotted in the lobby. But the truth was the quiet of her room felt too heavy. Too much space for thoughts she wasn't ready to unpack.

Ruth and Walter stood at the hearth with Evan, who held a coil of orange extension cord and a lantern dusted with ash. The weather radio murmured low and insistent.

"They say it'll be here in an hour or so," Walter said when he noticed Lila joining them. "Don't worry. We're ready."

Ruth handed Lila a mug without asking what she wanted. Steam rose in a thin, steady curl. Cinnamon and black tea filled the space between them.

"Thank you," Lila said, wrapping both hands around the warmth.

Ruth studied her for a moment, then said quietly, "Some people come to Midwinter because they're run-

ning. Some people come because they want to stop running. Which one are you?"

Lila lifted the mug and breathed in the steam like
courage. "I might be both."

Ruth smiled, as if that were answer enough.

Across the room, Evan checked the lanterns one by one,
methodical and precise. When he looked up, his gaze met
Lila's and held. Not prying. Not curious.

Aware.

Outside, snow lifted and fell in restless sheets. Night
would come early.

The storm wasn't just weather anymore. It was a
boundary.

Lila tightened her grip on the mug and felt the weight
of the quiet settle around her, heavier now. Roads would
close. Messages would go unanswered. Whatever waited
for her beyond this place would have to wait longer.

Chapter 2

The first real wind hit soon after dinner. It pressed against the windows and made the old beams groan. Evan stood in the foyer, one hand on the window frame, and watched the storm build until the world beyond the porch vanished into white. The lantern above the steps swung in the wind, its light flickering across the snow.

He could feel it in the air, the shift before a blizzard that made the skin on his neck tighten and his jaw lock. He'd learned to read weather the way other men read faces. Most people talked about storms as interruptions. For him, they were company. Predictable. Honest.

Behind him, the lodge creaked in the familiar way it always did when the cold moved in—pipes ticking, wood expanding. Juniper jumped onto the counter and began to clean her paws with deliberate disdain, pausing only when the wind howled.

Walter snored softly in his armchair near the fire with a newspaper collapsed over his chest. Ruth had retired upstairs with a novel and a promise to assist if needed. That left Evan alone in the quiet glow of lamplight, making his usual rounds.

He picked up his worn leather tool pouch and crossed to the back hall, checking every lantern one last time. Snow beat steady against the windows now, and the temperature had dropped enough for frost to creep along the glass.

He liked this part, the steady rhythm of keeping things running. The rest of life might be complicated, but this was simple. Tighten the bolts, refill the oil, keep the heat steady. Make sure people were safe.

He paused when he reached the laundry room. Someone had already stacked the quilts in neat piles by color. Blue, cranberry, cream.

He smiled under his breath. Lila Moore. The guest who offered to help between sips of chicken broth.

He hadn't expected her to follow through. Most people offered help to sound polite. She'd offered because she needed to feel useful. He recognized that instinct. He recognized the hunger under it, too, the quiet plea to be worth something when no one was clapping.

Pretty, too, though that wasn't what caught him first. It was how she looked at the world—alert, cautious—like someone stepping off a moving train and bracing for the platform to shift. The look tugged at a memory he didn't like touching.

A hospital hallway that smelled like bleach. A nurse saying his name like she hoped he wouldn't answer.

He shut the thought down and kept moving.

He stepped into the back hall and opened the exterior door long enough to check the path to the generator was clear. Cold bit his knuckles before he shut it out again.

When he returned to the lobby, she was there, curled into one of the chairs near the fire with a blanket wrapped around her shoulders and a notebook balanced on her knees. The lamp beside her cast a soft halo over her hair.

He stopped in the doorway and waited a moment before speaking. He didn't want to startle her. He didn't want to break whatever fragile calm she'd managed to build. "Snow's piling up now."

She looked up, and the fire reflected in her eyes. For a split second, it was someone else looking back at him. He looked away before the image could settle.

"The wind's really blowing," she said, as if saying it aloud might contain it.

"You warm enough?"

She nodded. "Ruth's quilts work miracles." She closed her notebook partway. "Do you ever get used to how quiet it is here?"

"You stop noticing after a while." He nudged a log back into place with the toe of his boot, needing the anchor.

"I'm not sure I want to stop noticing," she said. "It feels peaceful."

"Peaceful's one word for it. Lonely's another."

She tilted her head. "You sound like you know both."

"I do." He should have stopped there. Instead, he added, "I lost someone. Not all at once. Slowly."

Her sympathy came clean, without pity. "I'm sorry."

He shrugged. "Not your fault." But her voice softened the room anyway, and it made something in his chest loosen before he could stop it. He shifted the log again, then straightened. "What about you? What brings you here in the middle of winter?"

"Burnout," she said. "I write about places like this, but somewhere along the way I forgot how to enjoy them. Too many filters. Not enough truth." She hesitated. "And I needed to get out of reach before I read the rest of what people are saying about me. People can be cruel when there's a screen between them and the person they are criticizing."

That landed harder than it should have.

"So you came here to remember how to breathe."

She let out a breath that almost laughed. "That's the plan."

"You'll survive," he said. "The social media withdrawals don't last forever."

"That's what Ruth said."

"She's usually right."

The power flickered once. Both of them looked up.

"We'll lose it at least once before morning," he said. "Your room's ready. Lantern by the bed. Fireplace stocked. Generator's standing by."

"Thank you." She traced the edge of her notebook. "Do you ever want to leave this place?"

He shook his head. "I tried. Too much noise. Too many opinions that didn't mean anything."

"Like the internet."

"Exactly."

A log collapsed in the hearth, scattering sparks. He settled it without hesitation.

She watched his hands. "You're good at that."

"I've had practice."

"I think I'd like to learn."

He paused long enough to process her words. "Building fires?"

"Keeping them steady."

"You start by paying attention."

"To what?"

"Everything." He shouldn't have looked at her when he said it.

She smiled, softer now. "I'll remember that."

Outside, the wind rose, rattling the shutters. He tested the door latch once more. "You should get some sleep."

"In a bit. I like it here."

He stepped back before she could answer, already turning toward the hall.

The space between them returned too quickly.

"Right," she said after a beat, the word careful. "Of course."

By the time he realized what he'd done, she was already pulling the blanket tighter around her shoulders, quiet restored like a door gently closed.

The lodge was warm.

Evan had never felt the space feel colder.

He didn't answer right away. Instead, he crossed to the window and shifted the curtain edge, just enough to check the white-out. Then he stayed there a second longer than necessary, as if he were listening for something that wasn't the storm.

When he turned back, he didn't go to the tools. He stopped beside her chair, close enough that he could feel her heat without touching her.

"You'll hear the lodge creaking as the temperature drops," he said quietly, "so if you wake up and you're not sure what you're hearing, don't worry. This old place is sturdy. But if you need anything, don't hesitate to find me."

The words should have felt practical. Instead, they felt personal. It wasn't his place to reassure the guests. Ruth did that. But for some reason, Evan didn't want this woman to have one more thing to worry about.

"If it gets cold, let me know," he continued. "I'll stoke the fire."

"It's not the cold I'm worried about," she admitted.

He went still. "Then what is it?"

She hesitated, gaze dropping to the blanket edge where her fingers worried the fringe. "That I'll finally be quiet long enough to hear myself."

His throat worked once. "Yeah," he said, voice lower. "That part can be rough. But sometimes it's necessary."

For a beat, neither of them spoke. The fire popped softly. Walter snored. The storm pressed its face to the glass.

"Goodnight, Evan."

He hesitated. "Goodnight, Lila."

Upstairs, the wind followed him down the hall. When the power flickered again—longer this time—his stomach dropped.

One.

Two.

The lights came back.

He didn't move right away.

Because now he wasn't thinking about the storm.

He was thinking about what would happen if the safety he'd promised her failed. She hadn't asked him to care about her troubles, but for some reason he did. And he wasn't sure if he liked that or not.

Chapter 3

The storm hadn't stopped. The sun rose on snow piled in deep drifts and every tree outside the window looked frosted. Lila stood at the window next to her bed, cup of coffee warming her hands, and watched slow, patient flakes fall. The wind had quieted for now, but she knew better than to assume it would stay that way.

The quiet felt deeper after sleep. This wasn't the kind of silence she could scroll away from. Somewhere in the lodge, floorboards creaked under a careful step. Someone whistled a low, tuneless song she guessed belonged to Walter.

Another step followed—heavier, slower. *Evan*, she thought without meaning to. The realization came with a strange sense of orientation, like knowing where north was without checking a compass.

She turned back to the room, half expecting to see a glowing notification light on her nightstand. Old habit.

But the only thing that glowed was the lantern Ruth had left, its small flame flickering in its glass chimney.

Her laptop bag sat beside her suitcase near the door. She had meant to leave it closed to prove she could, but the longer she stared at it, the more her fingers itched. Checking her messages from clients wouldn't hurt anyone. Just a peek.

She knelt and unzipped the bag. The familiar click of the latch made something inside her ease. The screen woke to the last saved image—a blank document titled *Post Draft 314*. Beneath it sat a notification banner she hadn't opened yet. A subject line she recognized. A name she'd been avoiding.

She didn't click it.

No internet. The signal bars hovered empty in the corner. When she clicked the Wi-Fi icon, it searched for a network. Nothing. She tried again, this time holding her breath as if that might help.

Nothing.

She shut the lid with a snap and muttered, "Okay, universe. I get it."

A soft thump came from behind her. When she turned, she saw Juniper perched on the bed with the regal air of someone about to claim property. She had joined Lila in her room after breakfast and had claimed a spot on the dresser. Now, the cat's golden eyes flicked to the laptop bag, then to Lila, then back to the bag.

"No," Lila said. "Don't even think about it."

Juniper thought about it, and then sauntered across the blanket, tail high, and hopped down to the floor. Her paws made no sound, only purpose. In one smooth motion, she slid herself halfway into the open laptop bag.

"Hey!" Lila lunged, but Juniper was already curling inside the padded sleeve like she'd found a custom-built throne. A low purr rumbled through the fabric.

"That's not yours," Lila said, hands on her hips. "That's for...well, it *was* for work."

Juniper blinked lazily.

"You're mocking me, aren't you?"

The cat yawned, then tucked her paws under her chest. She looked perfectly at home, eyes closing to half-mast.

Lila sighed and surrendered. "Fine. You win. The weather made the decision for me."

A knock sounded at the door, three quick raps.

"One second!" She stepped over Juniper, who didn't budge, and smoothed her hair before she could stop herself. The reflex annoyed her. She hadn't done that for anyone in months.

When she opened the door, cold air spilled from the hallway, followed by Evan.

He stood there with snow melted on his jacket shoulders, his dark hair damp from the weather. She noticed, absurdly, that the cold clung to him while he didn't seem bothered by it at all. The sight of him had the same grounding effect as the smell of coffee or the sound of firewood splitting.

He carried an armful of split logs against his chest, bark dusted with snow, his gloves darkened with melt.

"Brought up another load," he said. "Figured we'd want it close."

"Oh." She followed his gaze to the hearth, where the wood bin was already fuller than it had been earlier. "That's smart."

He set the logs down carefully, stacking them with the same deliberate care he used for everything else. Then he nodded toward the bag at her feet. "You always travel with that much gear?"

She hesitated. "Occupational hazard. You never know when something will need to be documented."

He raised an eyebrow. "Even in a blizzard?"

"Especially in a blizzard. People love storm photos."

"You mean used to love storm photos," he said dryly. "There's no internet, remember?"

She crossed her arms. "I can still appreciate good light without posting it."

His mouth twitched, almost a smile, not quite. He liked that she pushed back, he realized—and then immediately told himself that liking it was a bad idea.

"If you say so." He set her suitcase near the wall. "We'll probably lose power for a bit tonight if the lines ice. Might be smart to unpack whatever you need before that."

She nodded. "Good to know. I'll..." She trailed off when she realized Juniper had emerged from the laptop bag and was winding between Evan's boots.

He looked down, then crouched automatically, one big hand extended. "There you are."

The cat sniffed his fingers, then butted her head into his palm, purring loud enough to be heard over the hum of the heater.

Juniper flopped over and displayed her belly in full trust. Evan rubbed behind her ear, and Lila had the fleeting, mortifying thought that she wouldn't mind trading places with the cat.

She pushed that thought aside fast enough to make herself blush.

"So," he said, standing again. "You settling in?"

"I think so. My phone has no signal, my laptop's been claimed, and the internet's dead. I might have to open a book."

"Sounds like success."

"It sounds like withdrawal." She gestured toward the bag. "Apparently, Juniper's determined to keep me from getting too much work done."

Evan's laugh was quiet but genuine. It softened the sharpness in his eyes and made the corners crinkle. She wondered, abruptly, whether he always looked this contained—or if the lodge kept parts of him hidden, the way it was starting to do for her.

"Smart cat."

Lila smiled despite herself. She wondered if he thought she was ridiculous. Or fragile. Or just another guest who'd leave once the novelty wore off.

"You're enjoying this."

"Watching you try to live without Wi-Fi? It's a good show."

She mock-glared at him. "You think I can't handle it?" The question came out sharper than she meant.

He met her gaze head-on, a hint of amusement in his voice. "I think most people panic when they realize they can't check their social media every ten minutes."

"Well, some of us like to be informed before venturing into a blizzard."

"You're not venturing anywhere. Roads are closed."

She frowned at him. "You enjoy being right, don't you?"

"Only when it keeps people alive."

Their eyes met, and for a heartbeat, the air between them felt different—warmer than the fire, sharper than the cold. Evan felt it too, and immediately stepped back, giving her space she hadn't asked for but somehow needed.

Then he nodded toward her window. "If you need anything, knock on the door by the stairs. That's my room. I'll be checking on things every few hours."

"I'll try not to bother you," she said.

"You won't." The certainty surprised him. He hesitated, then added, "Most folks find the first full day hard. The quiet gets loud before it settles down. Sometimes it makes people leave."

She absorbed that, realizing he was speaking from experience, not advice. "I'll keep that in mind."

He started to leave, then paused when Juniper gave a loud, possessive meow from the laptop bag. "Guess she's calling dibs."

"Apparently so."

"She'll win," he said. "She always does."

After he was gone, the door clicking softly behind him, Lila sat on the edge of the bed. The room felt smaller without his presence—still warm, but quieter in a way that made her aware of herself again.

And of him. The space he took up without trying. The way he'd looked at her like she was more than a complication in the weather.

She watched the cat curled smugly inside her bag and the dark screen of her laptop resting beside it. The irony of being trapped in a snowstorm while trying to escape her own didn't escape her.

Maybe the problem wasn't the silence—but who she was starting to notice inside it.

Juniper stretched and purred louder, as if in approval.

"Fine," Lila said softly. "You win again."

Chapter 4

By midday, the wind sliced through the pines and sent a fine mist of snow scudding sideways across the lodge grounds. Evan bent against it, coat zipped to his chin, breath fogging in short bursts. He checked the fuel gauge on the generator—three-quarters full after running for a few hours early in the morning—and tapped the metal once, satisfied.

He liked this kind of cold. It cleared the clutter from his mind, left room for thought. Everything was holding. For the moment.

He hadn't come back to Ember Lodge because it felt like home; he came back because after losing someone precious, he needed a place where expectations were few and silence didn't ask anything of him.

Behind him, the curtains opened in one of the second-floor windows. The Lake Room. Lila Moore's room. A figure moved past the glass, soft and deliberate. Even from this distance, he could tell she didn't quite know what to do with herself yet. He'd seen that kind of frustration before. City guests trying to adjust to stillness.

Except she wasn't pacing. She was moving slowly, as if testing the air.

He shook his head, smiling under his breath. "She's probably organizing her sock drawer just to stay busy."

Juniper appeared on the porch railing, tail flicking. The cat must have slipped out the kitchen door again. Evan clicked his tongue. "You're supposed to stay inside in weather like this, troublemaker."

Evan scooped her up and brushed snow from her fur.

"You know the rules," he said. "You think they don't apply to you."

The cat blinked slow, unimpressed.

"Fine," he said, tucking her under his arm. "One minute of fresh air, then back inside."

The snow came harder now—flakes the size of feathers. It was honest work. Check the systems. Fix what needed fixing. Keep people safe. The kind of effort where the result was simple. He scratched Juniper's ears for a minute while they appreciated the view.

Finally, he stepped inside, stamping snow from his boots.

Ruth called from the kitchen, "Everything holding?"

"For now," he answered. "I'll check again at dusk."

"Soup's on the stove if you get hungry," she said. "And keep that cat from sneaking out."

"Already caught her," he said, setting Juniper down. She immediately darted toward the hallway as if she'd been accused unfairly.

When Evan looked up, Lila was coming down the stairs. She had her hair pulled back in a loose braid and wore a thick cream sweater that slipped off one shoulder. The sight of bare delicate skin against thick fabric registered before he could stop it, a brief awareness he filed away and ignored. She stopped when she saw him, smile hovering somewhere between polite and shy.

"Everything okay out there?" she asked.

"So far," he said. "You warm enough?"

"Cozy, actually. I tried to go through my photos, but there's nothing to upload them to. It's weird, not being able to send things out into the world the second they exist."

"Maybe they can wait their turn," he said.

Her mouth curved. "You don't strike me as a man who rushes anything."

"Not if I can help it."

She took the last step down, glancing toward the kitchen where Ruth's voice hummed softly to herself. "Can I help with anything?"

He tilted his head. "You just volunteering to be useful?"

"Maybe."

The word carried more weight than it should have. He saw the question under it. Not *what can I do*, but *do I matter here*.

He thought about it. There wasn't much she could do outside—the storm was too heavy—but the wood bin near the hearth was half-empty. "You could help bring in some firewood. Just the small pieces. I'll grab the heavy stuff."

Her eyes lit with relief. Not pride. Gratitude. People who didn't know what to do with stillness usually liked having a task. He almost said no. Almost told her it would be easier if she stayed inside, warm and separate.

Instead, he nodded.

"Perfect," she said and slipped on the boots she'd left by the door and grabbed her coat.

He opened the door and let her step out first. The cold bit hard after the warmth inside. She drew in a sharp breath. "Wow. That's brisk."

"Montana brisk," he said. "Gets in your lungs, clears your head."

"Or freezes it solid."

He chuckled and handed her a pair of gloves from his pocket. "Here. You'll need these."

Their fingers brushed as she took them. Just a second. Enough for him to notice how cold her hands were—and how quickly she stilled when she realized he'd noticed.

They made their way to the covered woodpile beside the lodge. The snow muffled their steps and filled the silence between them until it felt companionable. He handed her a few small logs and watched her tuck them under her arm with determination. She wasn't the delicate tourist he'd assumed. A little out of her depth, sure, but not helpless.

Competent, he corrected. And quietly stubborn.

When she turned to say something, a lock of hair slipped free of her braid, dusted with snow. She blew at it and scowled, muttering, "Even the weather's against me."

He bit back a laugh. "It's not personal. The mountain treats everyone the same."

"Well, that's comforting," she said, straight-faced, and he had to look away before he smiled too openly.

Back inside, she knelt to stack the smaller pieces near the hearth while he carried in the larger logs. When she brushed snow from her sleeve, it landed in the firelight and melted instantly. Her breath fogged faintly as she worked, steady and uncomplaining.

"Thanks for the help," he said.

"You mean for not dropping the logs?"

"That, too."

She looked up at him, grinning. "You really thought I'd be one of those guests, didn't you?"

He raised a brow. "What guests?"

"The kind who shows up with impractical shoes and expects you to build them a fire while they film it for social media."

He gave a one-shouldered shrug. "You did arrive with two suitcases and a laptop bag."

"Which your cat now owns."

"That's her way of initiating you."

"Into what?"

"The order of people she barely tolerates."

Lila laughed, and the sound filled the place with easy warmth. Something in his chest shifted in response before he could stop it. "Guess I should be honored," she said.

"Could be worse," he replied. "She scratched the sheriff once."

That earned him another laugh, fuller this time.

They worked in silence for a while, the kind that didn't feel awkward. The fire popped, throwing off the smell of pine resin and warmth. When he finally straightened, brushing wood dust from his gloves, she was watching him again. Not in that way people look when they want something, but in the quiet, studying way of someone noticing the details.

He saw it then—not curiosity, not admiration, but something closer to trust.

He met her gaze, and something in her expression softened enough to make him wonder what she was seeing that he hadn't meant to show.

"Thanks," she said simply.

"For what?"

"For letting me help." *For not treating me like I'd break*, her eyes seemed to add.

He nodded once. "You did fine."

When she smiled, it reached her eyes this time.

Evan picked up his gloves and nodded toward the door. "I'll check the generator again before nightfall. You stay inside."

"Yes, sir," she muttered under her breath.

He caught it, smirked, and pulled on his hat. "Smart-mouth."

The door closed behind him with a muted thud, and the sound of her laughter followed him out onto the porch, chasing away the worst of the cold. Evan didn't turn around until the laughter faded, and by then the cold had nothing to do with the way his chest felt too tight.

Chapter 5

The snow turned from steady to relentless as the afternoon marched on, a quiet insistence that filled the space between breaths. Lila stood at the lobby windows with a dish towel in her hand from drying mugs, and watched the lake vanish behind a curtain of white. The world beyond the porch posts was only suggestion now. The lantern over the steps swung and tapped against its hook, a small metronome keeping time for the storm.

The phone behind Ruth's counter rang three times in a row. Not the chirp of a cell, not the cheerful trill of a shop, but the old landline bell that sounded like a memory. Ruth lifted the receiver, listened, and said a series of yeses that were not agreement so much as acceptance.

"I understand. This storm is forecast to drag on for some time, isn't it? We'll hold your deposit and shift your dates," she said. "You stay warm where you are. Midwinter will still be here."

Another call came before she finished marking in the guestbook. Then another. The cancellation script repeated, gentle and practiced. Ruth finished each one with reassurance and time, as if both were things she had in steady supply.

After the fifth call, she pressed the heel of her hand to her brow and exhaled. Walter slid a mug of tea to her elbow without asking.

"Well," he said lightly, glancing around the quiet lobby, "looks like it's you, me, and the cat."

Juniper flicked her tail from her place near the hearth.

Walter tipped his chin toward the back hall. "Plus Evan, who counts for at least two people when the wind gets too assertive."

"Three," Ruth said, patting the counter as if to anchor the room. "He is very good at storms."

Walter nodded toward the window. "Radio says the pass will likely close in the next hour."

Ruth didn't rush. She glanced at her list and made a small checkmark. "All right. Let's do a second pass." She spoke the way people do when the real work is already finished. "Lanterns topped off and set where we'll want them. Quilts redistributed. Water pots checked. Board games moved closer, in case we need a distraction later."

"I'll fetch the matches," Walter said, already moving. "And my patience for Scrabble."

Lila set the towel on the counter and rolled her sleeves. "Put me on a task."

Ruth's eyes warmed. "You're an easy guest to love." She tapped the list. "Lanterns first. Hallways and stair landings. Evan's outside. He'll want to know where you put the extras."

The knowledge that he was out there tugged something in her chest she didn't define. Not worry, exactly. Not yet. But awareness. Like the storm had a name now. She collected lanterns and the box of long matches and did as told. The hallways glowed one by one with small circles of gold. Glass chimneys clicked as they warmed. In the stairwell, the light made the old family photographs on the walls look animated. Lila's breath fogged the glass before clearing. Her reflection looked like a woman she recognized and not the professional persona she had constructed and maintained for years. She touched her own cheek as if the quiet were a physical thing she could steady.

By the time she returned to the lobby, the landline had stopped ringing. It sat, serene and heavy, as if it had not carried ten lives through the last ten minutes. Ruth had stacked playing cards and a cloth bag of wooden tiles on a side table. Juniper had claimed the bag and kneaded it with steady paws, purring like a generator in miniature.

"We are officially at what Walter calls a luxury occupancy rate: four humans and a very demanding cat," Ruth said.

Walter raised his palm for a high five. She gave it. The contact grounded her more than it should have.

The lights dipped. Not out, not even dramatically, but a soft sigh that made the hair lift along Lila's arms. The room held its breath. The lights recovered and the small sounds of the lodge resumed: water moving in the pipes, the stove ticking, a radiator clearing its throat.

"That will be the first warning," Ruth said, too calm to be truly worried. "It's like the house letting you know it might want attention."

Evan came in from the kitchen hall with his coat zipped and a knit cap pulled down low. He had that look again, concentration without hurry, attention narrowed to practical next steps. Snow clung to his shoulders and melted, darkening the canvas. He had a coil of extension cord over one shoulder and a flashlight in his hand though it was still daylight. He nodded to Ruth and Walter, then to Lila as if she were part of the lodge's inventory and therefore someone to keep track of. But his eyes stayed on her a fraction longer than they had to, as if confirming she was still here. Still steady. Still okay.

"Lines are icing," he said. "Gusts near the ridge are heavy. We'll probably lose power in the next hour. Generator's primed and I'll flip the switch if the main fails. Keep the load light, and we should be fine." His eyes flicked to the windows and stayed a heartbeat longer than they needed to, as if measuring the band of white between the porch posts. "If anyone calls, tell them to wait it out. The plow will go through when it's safe."

"Already done," Ruth said. "We are a fortress."

Evan's mouth tipped, not quite a smile. He moved to the hearth and used the poker to settle the wood into a structure that would burn steadily rather than showy. Lila watched the way his wrist rolled the metal, the way he balanced patience with purpose. He checked the draft, nudged a half-spent log into contact, stepped back to evaluate, then adjusted by a fraction. The fire responded, brightening and then settling into a calm, dependable glow.

"Teach me that later," she said before she could stop herself.

He glanced up. "What?"

"How to keep it steady like that." She felt silly, but it mattered. "I'm good at starting things. I don't always know how to tend them. Or when to stop pretending they're fine."

His gaze held hers a second longer than was comfortable, then softened. "All right," he said. "Later." His voice went quieter, like he'd made a promise to himself along with her.

The lights dipped again. This time they stayed dim half a beat longer and rose with a visible pulse, as if the current had heated through cold water. Ruth set her palm flat on the counter. Walter's hand found the back of her wrist the way a man finds a light switch in familiar darkness.

"Pots filled?" Evan asked.

"Two big ones," Ruth said. "And the kettle."

"Good," he said. "I'll do a run around the gutters."

Lila pictured a ladder in wind and tasted copper. "Do you need another set of hands?"

He was already moving, but he stopped, as if the question scratched a record. "You can help me by staying warm." His tone was practical, but his eyes held something firmer. Something that made her stomach tighten, not with annoyance but with the sharp awareness that he meant it. He didn't want her depending on him yet. "If the power goes and you get chilled, the whole system works harder. Blanket, tea."

"I can manage that," she said, trying not to feel like a child with a job chart. "What about after the gutters."

"After the gutters, you can tell me where you put the spare lanterns," he said, and the corner of his mouth turned up. "I'll pretend I knew all along."

Emotion moved through her in a fast, bright ribbon. This is how it is supposed to feel, she thought. Not grand gestures, not declarations, but a simple invitation to share a list.

He went into the white. The door closed on a gust and the sound of it knocked around the rafters before it settled. Lila crossed to the window and watched his shape move along the porch rail, then vanish into the smear. A dark figure against a world erased. It should have made him look small. It made her think of big things instead. Endurance. Steadiness. The kind of strength that does not need to be announced.

And the kind that never asked for anything back. Until now, when she realized she wanted to give him something anyway.

Ruth joined her with two mugs. "People who have not lived through winter think it is about waiting for spring," she said. "It is not. It is about learning to be yourself when the rest of the world disappears for a while."

"Is that why you stayed?" Lila asked. "After all these years."

Ruth's smile creased the fine lines around her eyes. "We stayed because love likes a place to live. This is ours. It could be yours for a week or two. A person can remember a lot in a few weeks."

The lights flickered a third time, then stabilized. Juniper's tail twitched as if she approved of the drama. Lila took her tea to a chair near the fire and tucked her feet beneath her to keep from pacing. She opened her notebook and drew the outline of the lantern over the door, then the shape of the porch posts, then the world beyond them that refused to stay contained within lines. When she lifted her head, snow feathered sideways. She imagined the lake under the blur and the way wind scored its surface. Evan's figure reappeared at the edge of vision, a ghost made of wool and resolve, then disappeared again.

She hated how quickly she started counting the minutes. Like the storm had taken something from her the moment it took him from the room.

When the power went out, it was not a bang or a theatrical sigh, but a clean click. The hum of the refrigerator ceased. The lights dropped. The room inhaled. For half a breath Lila heard only the storm and the soft clink of glass in the lantern chimneys.

Then the generator took. A breath later the lamps came back at half their previous wattage and the boiler kicked with a polite cough. The room exhaled as one organism. Lila realized she had been holding her breath for more than the power outage.

"Good boy," Walter said to the ceiling, as if the lodge were a dog who had returned when called. "Knew you'd remember how."

"Automatic transfer works," Ruth noted, checking the time and jotting a small star on her list. She didn't hurry. She looked like a person who had made a thousand lists in storms and understood that a star on the page meant steady as much as it meant success.

The kitchen door swung wide and Evan came in with a blast of cold, his cap dusted white, cheeks raw with wind. He stripped off his gloves and placed them on the stone hearth to steam. His eyes did a quick inventory of the room—Ruth, Walter, Lila, the cat, the lanterns, the level of the wood bin. Only after that did his posture drop a fraction from ready to ready-enough.

When his gaze landed on Lila, it lingered. Relief, quick and unguarded. He masked it a beat later, but she saw it anyway.

"Transfer worked," he said, echoing Ruth as a confirmation. "I'll keep it light. No space heaters. No hairdryers."

Ruth lifted her silver brows. "You have a history with hair dryers during storms?"

"One," he said. "It was memorable."

Walter chuckled. "The sheriff's wife wanted a blowout before a charity breakfast," he told Lila. "Evan nearly rewired the county explaining why not."

Juniper made an unimpressed chirp and climbed into Lila's lap without asking permission. The warmth and weight of the cat were immediate and total. The purr revved like a small engine. Lila's shoulders dropped. Her breath slowed. Outside, the storm pushed at the windows, insisting. Inside, something in her found the right speed and stayed there.

Evan crouched at the hearth to check the fire again. He set a log with the same neat economy he brought to the rest of his work and watched it take. Without looking up he said, "You put the extra lanterns in the hall closet by the dining room, right?"

She smiled. "Top shelf, left side."

He nodded once. "Thought so."

Their eyes met over the shoulder of the room and held. There was no dramatic exchange, only the quiet certainty that grows when two people do small things well in the same space. She looked away first because it felt like more than a look, and because she was not ready for more.

Evan's mouth parted, as if he meant to say something. *I'm glad you're here*, it almost seemed to shape itself.

But Ruth shifted a pot lid in the kitchen, and he closed his mouth, swallowing the words like they were heat he didn't know what to do with.

The storm deepened. Afternoon dissolved into a false twilight that arrived at least an hour early. Ruth declared soup a necessity and produced a pot that smelled like carrots, thyme, and the kind of broth that nurses people from the edge of colds and long days. They ate at the low table near the fire, bowls balanced on their knees, spoons clinking in a rhythm of comfort. Even Juniper's gaze softened toward generosity when Walter dropped a piece of bread crust for her with a wink and a solemn shh.

Between mouthfuls, they listened to the generator hum. Lila realized she had been absorbing the shape of Evan's movements—the way he rose without haste, the way he checked windows and doors, the way he measured the room the way a carpenter measures a board before the cut. She could not remember the last time she had watched someone be good at something and let that be the whole point. Not for content. Not for a caption. Only because it felt like witnessing competence was a form of grace.

After supper, Ruth sent Walter up to rest with the threat of a losing Scrabble rematch if he returned too soon. She shooed Lila into a blanket and insisted she sit still as if stillness were a task on the list. Evan disappeared and reappeared in cycles that matched the weather's breath. At last he stood near the window and watched the white for a long minute, hands on his hips, head slightly tilted the way it had been the night before when he listened for the storm's approach.

"Will it get worse?" Lila asked, quietly so the question didn't sound like doubt.

"Yes," he said. "Then better." He flicked a glance at her. "It always does."

A long, slow gust leaned into the house. Lila looked down at the cat asleep in her lap and traced a finger along the small divide between Juniper's ears. She thought of the people who would be scrolling and posting and complaining about traffic, and she didn't feel superior to them or sorry for herself. She felt something simpler. Present. Not a performance. Not proof. Only a woman in a chair with a warm cat and a view of white.

Evan turned from the window as if the storm had told him a story and he was satisfied with the ending. He lifted one of the lanterns from the sill and set it on the floor near Lila's chair, adjusting the flame until the light pooled at her feet The gesture made no sound and required no comment, but she felt it anyway. Not as comfort alone. As presence. As something she might start to rely on if she wasn't careful.

"Thank you," she said.

He stared at her. "You're welcome." The words were plain. The way he looked at her wasn't.

The lights wavered once more and held. The wind shouldered the porch. The house answered with heat and wood and the low, steady work of flame. Lila closed her eyes for a moment and listened to the harmony of it. In the dark behind her lids, she saw the lake under its white veil, the path to the maintenance shed half-buried, the careful tracks of a cat who didn't care for rules. She saw the outline of a man on a ladder, steady against the wind.

When she opened her eyes, the snow had thickened to the kind that erased even the suggestion of a horizon.

And for the first time since arriving, Lila wondered not how long she would stay—but what part of her might not want to leave. And what it would cost her if she did.

Chapter 6

By evening, the wind had taken on that hollow note that meant the worst of it had arrived. It moved over the roof in long, low breaths and then came back around from the north with a sharper edge, like a saw turned sideways. Evan stood on the porch and watched the snow sweep across the lake in white sheets, then disappear as if swallowed whole. The lantern over the steps swung and clicked. He counted the beats without thinking. Habit. A way to mark that the house and the weather were still talking to each other.

The generator hummed in the distance. He lifted his hand to test the air, palm open, as if the wind might put something in it. Temperature was dropping. Ice would continue building on the lines. He filed that under next checks and went back inside.

The lobby met him with steady light and honest heat. The fire held the way he wanted it to hold. Not flashy. Not racing through wood like a teenager on a dirt road. Banked and working. Ruth had left a pot of stew on the back of the woodstove with a ladle and a note that said, *Eat whenever the mood strikes.*

Walter's snores threaded in from the reading room like a distant saw on soft wood. The sound made him want to fix things. Every sound did.

Lila sat in one of the low leather chairs with Juniper sleeping in a tight gray comma against her thigh. She had a notebook open on her knee and a pencil tucked into the bend of her fingers. She wasn't writing. Just watching the fire. Her expression had smoothed into something he recognized in people who had made it through the first wall of quiet. Less braced. More here.

The sight of her like that hit him in the soft part of his chest. Not because she looked pretty. Because she looked settled. Because he'd started wanting to be the reason she could.

"Gutters are clear," he said, partly to let Ruth know when she came back down, partly because saying it out loud put a checkmark on the work in his head.

Lila's gaze slid from the flames to him. "Do you check them every hour?"

"When it's like this." He hung his coat on the peg near the door and set his gloves to steam on the stone. "Ice creeps. You keep after it or it keeps after you."

"That sounds like a life rule."

"It is," he said. "Doesn't always work with people. Works with gutters."

She smiled at that. The kind that reached the eyes and stayed there for a second before moving on. He felt it like a hand pressed into the center of his chest and then gone.

He made a slow circle of the room, listening to the lodge the way you listen to an old truck. He put a palm to the radiator by the window and felt for steady heat. He checked the gap at the back door to be sure the draft stopper sat snug. He shifted a log in the fire with the poker and watched the flame lean into the new route like a shoulder into wind. When he looked up, Lila was watching his hands again.

"You said you'd teach me," she said. She sounded like she knew it was not the time for lessons and yet wanted one anyway. He remembered the promise from earlier and nodded toward the hearth.

"Pull your chair closer," he said. "Blanket around your shoulders. You'll want to feel what the fire is doing, not just look."

She rose carefully so the cat kept sleeping and moved the chair into the edge of the hearth's warmth. He crouched and handed her the poker. His fingers brushed hers and a spark shot up his arm. Not fire. Not shock. Something like recognition. He moved his hand away and showed her the small notch where the metal bent.

"Balance is the whole thing," he said. "If you feed it too much, it races and collapses. Too little, it smothers. You listen. You look for how the wood is catching."

"Listen to fire," she said with a quiet laugh. "That sounds like poetry."

"It's just work," he said. "Watch the blue at the base. That tells you how hot she is."

She leaned in and mirrored his posture. He pointed to a log that had burned down to a glowing bridge and another that had propped against it and refused to catch.

"Slide the stubborn one half an inch to meet the coals here," he said. "Then give the bottom a touch more air. Not too much."

She moved the poker, careful and slow. The log shifted with a soft scrape. He waited through three heartbeats. The blue at the base pulsed brighter, then steadied. The reluctant log lifted into flame like a person who had finally decided to stand.

"There," he said.

Her breath caught in a small sound he treasured from people learning to do a thing their hands had never done before. Not pride. Not surprise. That thin note between. "I see it," she said. "Thank you."

He nodded. The word did something in his chest again. He stood to ease the pressure in his knees and rolled his shoulders while she watched the fire as if it might do another trick. It wouldn't. Not right now. Fires are like people that way. Once they give you one good thing, they expect to rest.

"It's not really about the fire," he heard himself say, and the words surprised him with their own honesty.

Lila looked up. "What is it about, then?"

He stared at the flames like they might answer for him. "About not forcing it," he said carefully. "About showing up when it matters. About not walking away the first time it gets messy."

Her throat moved. She didn't look away. That was the dangerous part. "And if you do walk away?" she asked, voice quiet. "If you leave it alone too long?"

He swallowed. "Sometimes it goes out," he said. "Sometimes it leaves coals under ash. Either way, you don't get to pretend it didn't happen."

The lights dipped, then went out with a clean click.

He listened as the generator picked up torque, a low throat-clearing sound that told him the automatic transfer had engaged.

This time he didn't wait to see if it would right itself. He grabbed his hat.

"I'll check the shed," he said. "I'll come," she said, and started to set the poker down.

"Stay," he said. Not unkind. It came out more like a plea than he meant. "It's slick on the path. I'll be two minutes."

He didn't add the rest, the part that lived under his ribs: *I don't want you out there where I can't keep you safe.*

She sat back and folded the blanket tighter instead of arguing, which he appreciated. Some people heard no as small betrayal. She heard it as a promise to return.

He stepped into hard wind and went around the side of the lodge into the chalk-gray light. The shed squatted against the bank like a bear with its back to weather. He knocked snow from the latch and opened the door to the smell of oil and warm metal. The generator chugged steady. He put a hand to the housing the way he always did. It gave back a little vibration. He checked the line. No ice.

He tightened a connection he had already tightened once today and then stood for a second with his eyes closed and listened.

He shouldn't be thinking about her out here. He should be thinking about amperage and fuel and ice. But the quiet had made room for the truth, and the truth was he'd started building his evenings around the sound of her voice.

That was the kind of wanting that got you hurt.

When he came back in, his hat rim held a ring of frozen crystals that he brushed off on the porch.

Lila's chair was where he'd left it, the cranberry quilt folded neatly across the seat as if she'd just risen from it. Juniper had abandoned her post and claimed the warm spot on the rug where a patch of sun would be if the sky knew what sun was.

"All right," he said. "She's fine."

"Good," she said. The relief in her voice was small but true.

Lila realized then it hadn't been the generator she'd been worried about. The understanding settled as she lifted the ladle from the pot on the stovetop and poured stew into two bowls without asking if he wanted any. She handed him one as if he lived here.

He did live here. Still. It felt new, the way she did it.

They ate with bowls balanced on their knees and the fire complaining in little pops. Ruth drifted down for a while with a book and a sweater thrown over her nightgown, then back up again after a round of "you two don't let the house blow away." Walter snored and woke and snored again and finally gave up and shuffled into the lobby with his newspaper only to sit and watch the snow once he got there, paper forgotten.

"Where were you headed before you came here?" Evan asked Lila when their bowls were empty and the lull of stew and heat made conversation easy.

She looked surprised that he wanted to know. People didn't often ask her questions that were not covered by a bio on a website. "Nowhere, honestly," she said. "Which is part of the problem. I was everywhere and nowhere. I had a list of places to go this spring. Marrakech. Tulum again. A train across Canada. They sounded good when I said them out loud." She hesitated, mouth opening as if to add something more, something sharper. "None of them felt like home."

"What does feel like home?" he asked.

She glanced at the window, where white pressed its face against the glass. "That's a dangerous question in a storm," she said lightly, tipping her head toward the wind. "I think the weather might have opinions."

He caught the shift. The pause. The way she'd stepped sideways instead of forward. He let it go. "Weather usually does," he said.

"I don't know yet," she added, settling back into the chair. "That's the answer I came here to find."

He held her gaze for a beat and then nodded like a man stamping a word into soft metal. Accepted. "You'll know it when you start building it," he said.

"And if I don't?"

"You will," he said. "Most people do when they start telling themselves the truth."

She looked down at her hands. "That part's the hard part."

"Hard's not the same as complicated." It came out rough, but he meant it as comfort.

She smiled a little. "You say things like that and I feel like I should write them on a card and pin it to a corkboard."

"Don't," he said. "Just do the thing."

Her laugh was soft. "Right. Just do the thing."

Another flicker passed through the lights. The generator caught again without fuss. He put his bowl on the nearby table and rose. "Loop," he said.

She nodded as if they had been doing this for years. "I'll hold the fort."

He made another rotation. Radiators. Windows. Back door. He tilted the blinds and peered into the white and could not even find the porch rail. The world had been erased down to lines of what mattered. Heat. Water. Light. People. He liked it when a storm did that. The abrasion of unnecessary things fell away and the grain of what was left showed through.

When he returned to the hearth, he found Lila writing after all. Not fast. Not the clatter of someone trying to keep up with a thought that wanted to get away. The kind of writing that looked like someone was listening to their own words as they arrived. She finished a line and closed the notebook with a palm flat to the cover, then set it aside.

"You ever read your own work out loud?" he asked.

She blinked. "Sometimes. Why."

"Because it sounds different when it hits air. Truth and performance make different shapes in a room."

She tilted her head. "I might do that later. Not to an audience."

"Good," he said. "The cat's pretty harsh."

"Juniper would heckle me."

"She'd leave mid-sentence if it bored her."

They let the quiet fill back in. The hush was not empty. It hummed with the sound of a building doing its job in weather it respected. Pipes. Flame. The steady engine outside. Walter finally drifted off with his chin on his chest and Ruth returned with more blankets and tucked one around his knees without waking him. Marriage looked like that to Evan. The small ways people kept each other warm.

He found himself thinking: I could do that. I could keep someone warm.

And just as quickly: Not her. Don't reach. Don't make her the thing you lean on.

A sharp bang from somewhere above made him lift his head. Not power. Not the generator. He knew those noises the way a fisherman knows the difference between a wave and a whale. This sounded like a shutter gone loose or a branch hitting siding. He stood.

"Stay here," he told Lila. "I'll be right back."

She nodded once and didn't ask if she could help. That was trust he had not earned and still took as a gift. He went up the stairs two at a time, then slowed at the landing to listen. The second-floor hallway held the chilly feeling of air sneaking in where it shouldn't. He searched room by room until he found the window that had rattled open a fraction at the latch. Ice had built at the frame and kept it from sealing. He shoved gently and then with more weight until the wood gave and the sash fell into place. The wind eased at once. He checked the radiator under the sill. Warm. He lingered until the room felt like a room again rather than a mouth letting weather in.

On his way back down, he stopped outside the Lake Room and looked toward the lake out of reflex. Nothing to see but white. Still, he stood for a second in the dim and let the shape of the world he knew fill in the blanks. Trees. Shore. The far ridge. The spot where the sun came up in summer. The path to the maintenance shed. The drift that always formed where the porch steps met the lower walk. He could walk it blind. He often had.

He thought of her upstairs. Of her hands on the poker. Of her listening instead of performing. And the thought came, simple and terrifying: I don't want this to be temporary.

He came back to the lobby and found that Lila had not moved far. She sat in the same chair with the same blanket, but her face had changed. Less pretense. More steadiness. She looked like a person who had decided to try something and meant it.

"Window," he said. "It's fixed."

"Good," she said. "We would hate to let all the expensive heat out."

"Ruth would make me sleep with the shovel."

"She would not." Lila smiled toward the stairs. "She'd tuck you in with two quilts and then bring you stew."

"True," he said. "The quilts would smell like cedar and victory."

"Victory," she echoed, and the word landed between them like a secret.

A fresh gust hit the front of the lodge hard enough to make the beams give a small groan. He checked the lantern above the steps out of reflex. It swung and clicked, regular as a heartbeat. He exhaled some piece of worry he hadn't named.

"You tired?" he asked.

"A little," she said. "But also not. I don't want to miss it."

"There's nothing to see," he said. "That's kind of the point."

"I mean I don't want to miss being here for it."

He watched her for a long moment. Most guests wanted to be somewhere else in the middle of a storm. Even locals sometimes did. She wanted to sit with it. He respected that more than he could say without sounding like a fool.

"Lila," he said, and her name came out rougher than he meant.

She stilled. "What?"

He took a step closer before he realized he'd done it. Close enough to feel the warmth of her blanket, close enough to feel how much he wanted to take the cold from her hands with his own.

"Nothing," he said too fast.

He almost said: *You make this place feel different.*

He almost said: *I'm glad you're here.*

But Walter shifted in his sleep and the floorboard popped, and Evan backed up like the room itself had reminded him of the line he was trying not to cross.

"Sit," he said instead. "We'll keep the fire honest and let the wind talk. That's the job."

"That's the job," she repeated.

He slid a small log onto the coals and made the slight adjustment that kept the flame from running too fast. She watched and then reached for the poker without asking. He handed it over. Her knuckles brushed his thumb. Heat took the stubborn bit of wood. The light came up a fraction and settled.

She didn't pull her hand away right away. Neither did he.

It wasn't a touch that meant anything by itself. It was a touch that threatened to mean something if they let it.

They stayed like that as the evening ran itself down. Ruth drifted off upstairs again after checking the list and drawing a star in the margin for nothing except the fact they were all still here. Walter muttered in his sleep and smiled, the way a man does when he dreams of years that were good and simple. Juniper resettled on the warm rug, extended one paw, and sighed in the pure contentment only a cat can manage.

Lila had tucked her legs under her and was writing again. When she noticed him watching, she set the notebook aside and tipped her head toward the fire.

"Do you ever feel proud of it?" she asked. "When it holds like this."

"Not proud," he said. "Grateful. Pride makes you relax when you shouldn't. Gratitude keeps you checking the corners."

She nodded as if she would write that down later. Maybe she would. He found he didn't mind the idea of showing up in her pages if the words were true. He just didn't want to be a chapter she left behind.

The clock on the mantle said a time that felt later than it was. Storm time stretches, then snaps back. He banked the fire for the night with the movements that lived in his muscles and gave Lila the small nod that meant we're fine for a while. She stood and smoothed the blanket, and he realized all at once how easy it had become to account for her in the room. Not a guest to manage. Not a complication. A person who made the space feel like it had a new corner that belonged.

"I'll sit up for another hour," he said. "Go rest. If you can't sleep, come back down. I'll be here."

She held his gaze and something clear moved through it. Trust, yes. Also a kind of answer to the unasked question of whether she would run from this place when the roads opened. Not yet. Maybe not at all.

And that hope, sudden and bright, scared her more than the storm did.

"Okay," she said. "Goodnight, Evan."

"Goodnight, Lila."

She crossed the lobby with the blanket folded over her arm, quiet as a person who had learned where the boards talk. At the bottom step she paused and looked out into the white and then back at him. He gave her a small salute with two fingers. She smiled and went up.

He sat in the chair she had left and let the heat of the cushion hold his back while the storm pressed its weight on the roof. The generator kept steady. The lantern over the porch tapped time. He listened to the house. He listened to the wind. He listened to the part of himself that stopped shouting two winters ago and learned to speak in a normal voice again.

It said: *Don't reach. She'll leave.*

And underneath that: You'll miss her in a way you don't get to call reasonable.

When he finally rose to make another loop, he felt the familiar ache in his knees and welcomed it. Work that made sense. A house doing what houses do. A storm that would be worse and then better. A woman upstairs who couldn't check the world even if she wanted to, learning what quiet demanded.

He took his hat from the peg and stepped into the cold. The wind greeted him like an old friend who has no use for small talk. He smiled into it and went on with the job.

Chapter 7

The power failed just after dawn, so quietly that for a moment Lila didn't notice. She woke to the muted blue of early morning, the kind of half-light that hides the edges of things. Her room felt different—too still. No hum from the boiler, no click from the radiator pipes. She pushed back the quilt and sat up, listening. The storm had softened into a whisper, but the air inside had cooled enough that her breath made a small cloud in front of her face.

She swung her legs out of bed and crossed to the window. The world outside was buried. Snow had drifted halfway up the porch railing, and the lake was a white sheet stretching to the far shore. The sky carried the faint gray promise of more weather, but for now, everything was calm. She rested her forehead against the glass. A day without the hum of electricity. No outlets. No internet. No way to know what was happening beyond the snow.

Her chest tightened at the thought. The silence felt exposed, like standing in the middle of a room with the lights on and nowhere to hide.

And beneath that fear—unexpected and unwelcome—there was something else.

Possibility.

And that scared her.

Because the quiet was starting to feel less like a break and more like a door she could walk through.

Then her stomach growled, shattering the fragile spell.

"Right," she said to herself. "Possibility comes later. Coffee comes first."

She pulled on jeans, socks thick enough to make her boots optional, and one of her softest sweaters. Downstairs, the lodge was lit by scattered lanterns. Their flames wobbled against the logs, painting the room in gold and shadow. Ruth stood near the woodstove in the kitchen alcove, spoon in hand, stirring something fragrant. The smell of thyme and onion filled the air.

"Morning, dear," Ruth said without looking up. "Welcome to the quiet kind of day."

"Power's out?"

"Since about six. Evan's been out to check the line already. The rest of us are reverting to the nineteenth century. Water's heating on the stove if you want to pretend the instant variety is real coffee."

Lila smiled, taking the tin mug Ruth offered her. "Pretending's my specialty."

"I had a feeling." Ruth winked. "He's out back if you want to tell him breakfast is ready. Though you might have to yell."

Lila hesitated, then nodded. She carried her mug to the door and pushed it open. The cold hit like a clean breath. Evan was by the generator shed again, half-buried in snow, dark jacket zipped to his throat, beanie pulled low. He was crouched, flashlight balanced between his teeth, one hand steady on a set of tools. The generator sat open, its metal guts gleaming with frost.

For a moment she watched him.

There was something intimate about seeing someone work when there was no audience. No performance. Just effort.

And the worst part was how quickly her body relaxed because he was there.

"Any luck?" she called.

He spat the flashlight into his hand and looked up. "Depends on your definition. It's not dead, but it's definitely sulking."

"So... moody?"

"Exactly. It's picking up bad habits from the cat."

She laughed, and the sound bounced off the porch posts. "Ruth said breakfast's ready."

"Good. Tell her to save me a bowl."

"You'll freeze if you stay out much longer."

"I've been colder," he said, then shut the generator's panel with a precise, final motion. "But you're right. I'm done arguing with it for now."

He brushed snow off his gloves and joined her at the door. When he stepped inside, the warmth hit his face, turning the tips of his ears pink. He smelled like pine and cold air. He set his gloves by the stove to dry, nodding at Ruth.

"You're not the only one who can coax miracles out of broken machinery," she said, handing him a bowl of steaming chili.

"I'm aware," he said, and gave her a smile that belonged more to the corner of his mouth than the rest of his face.

Lila took her own bowl and followed him into the dining nook. The table had been pushed closer to the woodstove for heat. Juniper was curled in a chair nearby, tail flicking lazily. The soup was hot and earthy—lentils, carrots, something smoky underneath. She hadn't realized how hungry she was until the first spoonful.

"Walter still asleep?" she asked.

"Out cold," Ruth said from the stove. "He and the cat are in a competition for who can snore louder."

Evan huffed a quiet laugh, the kind that came from deep in his chest. "My money's on Walter."

"Always." Ruth poured herself tea and took a seat. "I'll let you two mind the place for a bit. I promised Walter I'd bring him breakfast before he claims I've run off with his porridge." She disappeared down the hall, humming.

The moment Ruth left, the space shifted. Not awkward. Not empty. Just private in a way Lila wasn't used to anymore.

Lila eyed Evan over the rim of her mug. "Doesn't this get exhausting? The storms, the power outages, all this?"

He swallowed his bite, considering. "Not really. You can't fight weather. You just learn its rhythms."

"That sounds peaceful. Predictable."

"Sometimes." He stared into his bowl for a moment. "Other times it's like living with an unpredictable roommate. You get along fine until it decides to rearrange the furniture."

Lila smiled. "You sound like you've been here forever."

He shrugged, eyes fixed on the fire. "Close enough."

"You grew up in Midwinter, right?"

"Outside of town. My dad worked for the county road crew. I came to the lodge summers when Ruth and Walter needed help. Then one day I didn't leave."

"Didn't want to?"

"Didn't need to." His tone was easy, but something about the way he said it made her wonder if he was convincing her—or himself. "There's enough work to keep me busy. The Mercers are good people. Juniper tolerates me. Can't complain."

She studied him for a moment, tracing the quiet lines of his face. "I think I envy that. Knowing exactly where you belong."

He looked up. "You don't?"

Lila fiddled with her spoon. "I used to think I did. My work—writing, travel, the next project—was my whole identity. It made sense. Until it didn't."

"What changed?"

She hesitated, then gave the soft half-truth she'd rehearsed for months. "I stopped enjoying it. Too much time online, too many people telling me what to think, what to post, questioning my decisions and integrity. I wanted to disappear for a while. Now that I have…" She laughed quietly. "I feel like I've turned my back on my best friends."

Evan's eyes narrowed slightly. Not suspicion. Recognition. "That's not the whole thing. Something happened."

Her breath hitched. She forced a smile. "It's enough of it."

He didn't let her off the hook. He set his spoon down, slow and deliberate, like he didn't trust his hands to be casual. "No," he said quietly. "It's what you can say out loud."

The warmth from the stove suddenly felt too intimate. Too close. Lila's fingers tightened around her mug. It wasn't that she didn't trust him. It was that trusting him would make this real.

Outside, a gust scraped the window.

"I got in trouble," she said finally, voice low. "Not legal trouble. Just public." She swallowed. "I said something that got twisted. And then people decided to tear me apart for it. Nothing I do seems to be able to fix it. I'm tired of trying, but if I don't… I could lose everything I've built."

Evan's jaw flexed. His reaction was immediate, unguarded anger, and it wasn't at her. "You don't deserve that," he said.

The force of it startled her. "You don't even know what I said."

"I don't need to." His voice stayed controlled, but his eyes didn't. They were too sharp, like he wanted to go outside and fight the storm just to have something to punch.

"People who want a villain don't care about facts. They care about the feeling they get from throwing stones."

Lila blinked fast. Her throat burned. "That's exactly what it felt like."

He leaned back, dragged a hand down his face, and forced himself to soften. "Can it reach you here?"

She gave a small shrug. "No signal. No Wi-Fi. No comments." She tried to make it light. "It's the first time the noise hasn't been able to reach me."

His gaze held hers. "And when the roads open?"

The question landed like a crack in ice. Lila looked down at her bowl. "Then I go back."

His expression flickered. Not neutral. Not polite. Something that looked like disappointment he didn't want to admit to.

"I didn't mean for that to sound..." she started.

"Like you've already decided," he finished, and the words came out rougher than he meant. He cleared his throat, but the damage was done. He'd shown too much.

Lila's pulse kicked. This was the dangerous part Ruth hadn't warned her about. Not the storm. Not the power.

The way staying could start to feel like choosing.

Outside, the generator rumbled faintly in the distance, then stuttered and fell silent again. Neither of them moved to fix it. The silence that followed pressed in, heavy and expectant.

For a while, they sat like that—two people sharing heat and soup in a storm-muted morning. The fire cracked softly. Snow hissed against the windows. The world beyond was white and endless.

Lila drew her blanket tighter around her shoulders and looked at him through the flicker of light. "If we're stuck here awhile," she said, "I don't want to waste it."

Evan's eyes lifted. "Waste what?"

She opened her mouth. The truth pressed close, ready.

I came because I couldn't breathe. Because the stress was killing something in me. Because I don't know who I am without everyone watching.

Because being here with you feels like relief, and relief feels like temptation.

But she didn't say any of that. She swallowed and chose the safer version. "The quiet," she said.

Evan nodded once. "Then I'll teach you."

He stood and went to the stove, testing the soup pot with a wooden spoon. "We'll make it through fine. The generator will come back once the ice melts."

"You sound certain."

"I've seen worse storms."

She tilted her head. "And yet you continue to tough it out?"

He didn't answer at first. The firelight painted his profile in orange and gold. "I thought about it once," he said finally. "Years ago. My fiancée wanted to move to Helena. She said there wasn't enough life here. I told her we could make our own life."

He paused. "We never got the chance to find out who was right. She got sick before we could decide."

Lila felt the shift in his voice—subtle but real. The tone of someone who's learned to tell a painful story without letting it sting.

"I'm sorry," she said softly.

"It was a long time ago," he said. "She needed noise. I needed quiet. And then everything stopped."

Lila's chest tightened. Because she heard herself in that divide, and she hated it.

She wanted to say, *I'm not her.*

But she couldn't, because she didn't know if that was true.

And the not knowing made her want to run.

Instead, she said, "I think I came here for the opposite reason. I had too much noise and not enough quiet."

He looked at her then, a slow, measuring glance that felt more like understanding than judgment. "Don't let it make you disappear," he said, and the words came out before he could tame them.

Lila blinked. "I thought disappearing was the point."

His throat worked. He looked away, jaw tight, like he'd stepped too close to something tender. "Sometimes it is," he said. "Sometimes it's just avoidance with better lighting."

The air between them went sharp. Not angry. Charged.

He met her gaze. "You're starting to like it here," he said quietly. "And liking something doesn't make it safe."

Her heart thumped hard enough to make her feel foolish. "Why wouldn't it be safe?"

Evan's gaze dropped to her hands, then lifted again. "Because you'll leave," he said, and there was no edge to it. Just truth.

Lila stared at him. The simplest part of her wanted to say: Then ask me to stay.

The smarter part remembered that men didn't ask for things they couldn't afford to lose.

The generator coughed once, far off. The lodge held its breath. Then the sound died again.

Evan stood abruptly, as if he needed motion to keep from saying the next sentence. He crossed to the hearth and added a log to the fire with too much force. Sparks lifted and fell.

"Careful," Lila said, gentle.

He exhaled, slower. "Yeah."

The lantern on the counter wavered but held. Like the two of them, trying.

For the first time in a long while, Lila didn't feel capable of capturing the moment.

Not for an audience. Not for proof.

She just let it exist—firelight, warmth, quiet company, and the comfort of being nowhere except exactly where she was supposed to be.

And the fear that being exactly where she was supposed to be might change what she was supposed to do next.

Chapter 8

With late afternoon, the storm shrunk to a whisper—wind down to breath, snow easing from sheets to the slow, thoughtful drift of a shaken snow globe. The generator stayed silent, a quiet that felt provisional rather than safe.

Inside, the only sounds were the occasional pop from the woodstove and the rhythmic scratch of Juniper's claws on the braided rug as she stretched.

Evan sat near the hearth, sleeves rolled to his elbows, working a piece of sandpaper over the handle of a lantern that had lost its shine years ago. The motion was easy, repetitive, half meditation and half habit. He didn't really care if the brass gleamed; he just liked the quiet rhythm of making something right again. It kept his hands busy so his head wouldn't wander where it wanted to.

Across the room, Lila sat on the floor with her back to the couch, a notebook open on her knees. The light from the stove warmed her face, bringing a soft flush to her cheeks. She'd been writing for a while—pausing to think, jotting something, frowning, then smiling like she'd surprised herself. He hadn't asked what she was writing. He didn't need to. The act of it seemed to be the point. Watching her write felt like watching someone test their footing after a long fall. It was hard not to want to be part of that.

When she finally spoke, it startled him.

"I forgot what silence sounds like."

He set down the lantern. "Most people do."

"It's strange," she went on, eyes still on the page. "I used to think silence meant absence—like something was missing. But it's not empty."

"Full of everything you've been drowning out," he said.

She looked up at him. "Exactly."

He leaned back against the stone ledge of the hearth, rubbing the rough pads of his fingers together to dust away brass grit. "The first time I stayed through a storm alone, it was like that," he said. "Too much quiet. Drove me half crazy. After she was gone, I thought I wanted noise—but what I really wanted was proof that I wasn't the only one left."

"What happened?"

He shrugged. "Realized I was fine being the only one left." The lie in that sentence tasted familiar.

She smiled, faint but genuine. "That sounds lonely and peaceful all at once."

"It was." He paused. "Still is, sometimes." And it wouldn't be, if you stayed. He didn't let himself think the rest.

A log collapsed in the stove, sending sparks dancing against the grate. Lila watched the embers for a long moment, chin resting on her knee. "You said earlier you haven't left Midwinter in years. Was that by choice?"

He gave a quiet laugh. "That depends on who you ask."

"I'm asking you."

He looked toward the window, where the world outside had gone gray blue with evening. "There was a time I thought I'd travel. See what everyone else was rushing toward. But after—" He stopped. The air between them waited.

"After?" she prompted gently.

"My fiancée," he said finally. "She wanted out of this life. Out of here. I thought I could build something she'd want to stay for, but she left anyway." He rubbed a thumb along the edge of his lantern, catching the flicker of firelight on the metal. "I guess I stayed because leaving felt like admitting she was right. And because staying was easier than starting over." And because if he left, there would be nothing left to keep him steady.

"I'm sorry," she said softly.

He shrugged, but the motion was too slow to pass as indifference. "It's not a tragedy anymore. Just a story I tell when people ask why I haven't gone farther than the next ridge in a decade." He didn't add: It's the story I tell so I don't have to admit it still bruises.

"Does it ever get lonely?"

"Sometimes. But I've made peace with quiet." He met her gaze. "You learn a lot about yourself when there's nothing left to distract you." You also learn what you've been avoiding.

Lila closed her notebook, turning it over in her hands like she needed something to anchor her. "I thought I already knew myself. Turns out I only knew the version of me that fit into other people's expectations."

"Clients? Readers?"

"Everyone. I used to measure my worth by engagement stats. Enough to make a living. Enough to make mistakes public." Her laugh was small and brittle. "When the numbers dropped, I'd panic. Post more. Share more. Pretend harder. Somewhere along the way I forgot that I used to write because I loved it."

He studied her face in the shifting light. "You can start loving it again. Doesn't matter how long it's been."

She glanced up at him. "You really believe that?"

"I wouldn't still be fixing this place if I didn't." And I wouldn't still be sitting here if you weren't in this room.

The way she looked at him then—steady, unguarded—hit deeper than he expected. He wasn't used to being seen that way. Not as the guy who kept pipes from freezing or snow from blocking doors. Just as someone who stayed. Someone solid. Someone worth staying for.

"You make it sound easy," she said.

"It's not." He smiled, slow and self-deprecating. "But I've learned that easy things don't last long in the cold."

She laughed softly, the sound melting into the steady hiss of snow outside. For a while, neither of them spoke.

The storm whispered at the walls, and the fire did the talking for them.

Lila's fingers tightened around her notebook. "I didn't just get tired," she said, voice lower. "I got ripped apart."

He went still. "Lila."

She flinched like her name had weight. "It was one mistake. One sentence. And suddenly people had permission to hate me like it was a hobby."

Evan's jaw flexed. The heat in his eyes wasn't curiosity. It was restraint. "Do you want to tell me what you said?"

She shook her head quickly. "No. Because you'll hear it, and you'll decide I deserved it."

His chair scraped the floor as he stood. "Look at me."

She did, reluctantly, as if she was bracing for impact.

"I'm not your comment section," he said, voice controlled but rough at the edges. "And I'm not interested in judging you from a distance." He took one step closer, then stopped himself like there was a line taped to the floor. "You don't have to earn decency."

Her throat moved. "You say that like you mean it."

"I do." The words came out sharp. Personal. "I don't care what strangers did with your worst day." He exhaled, slower. "I care what it did to you."

Lila blinked fast. It was dangerously close to the truth she hadn't known she needed.

When Ruth appeared in the doorway, wrapped in a shawl, she looked between them and smiled the kind of knowing smile that made Evan consider retreating to the maintenance shed. Perfect timing, as always.

"I see you two haven't let the dark get you down," she said. "Walter's asleep again, bless him. I'm going to turn in before the temperature drops any further."

"Need anything before you do?" Evan asked, turning his tone into something safer.

"Just promise me you'll bank the fire before you call it a night. I'd rather not wake up to a chimney full of regrets."

"Got it."

Ruth squeezed his arm as she passed. "You always do." Her gaze flicked to Lila. Soft. Affirming. Like she was watching something take root.

After she disappeared upstairs, the silence settled again—different now, softer, shared. And heavier, because they'd almost said too much.

Lila shifted, drawing her blanket higher around her shoulders. "Do you ever get tired of being everyone's hero?"

He looked up, startled. "What?"

"You fix things. Keep the lights on. Hold this place together when everything else falls apart. Must be a lot of pressure."

He shook his head. "Not pressure. Just maintenance. Things need care or they stop working. Same with people." His eyes met hers. "And sometimes you don't realize someone's been running on empty until they finally sit down."

Her smile faded into something more thoughtful. "I don't think anyone's cared for me in a long time. Not really."

The words came out so quietly he almost didn't catch them. He didn't rush to answer. Sometimes silence was the kindest reply. Sometimes it was the only thing keeping him from saying the wrong honest thing.

After a while, he said, "You're here now. That's a start." He wanted to add: And I'm here. But that felt like a promise he wasn't sure he had the right to make.

She nodded, eyes glimmering in the firelight. "Maybe it is."

The logs settled again, throwing sparks up the chimney. He got up to bank the fire for the night. She rose too, holding the lantern while he arranged the coals and shut the iron grate. When he straightened, they were standing close enough that he could see the reflection of the flames in her eyes.

"Thank you," she said.

"For what?"

"For making it feel like we're not just waiting for the storm to end." Her voice caught. "Like I'm not just waiting to go back to being punished."

His chest tightened. "You're not," he said, too fast. Too certain. "Not here."

He didn't know how to respond to what he felt, so he did what he always did—worked. He adjusted the wick on the lantern in her hand, though it didn't need adjusting. His fingers brushed hers, and the touch sent a subtle, electric awareness through him. She didn't move away. Neither did he, for one breath too long.

For a long moment, they stood there in the warm glow—two people who had both built walls and somehow found themselves standing in the same open space. And the dangerous truth was that the open space felt like it could become home.

He cleared his throat. "You should get some sleep. It'll be colder by morning."

She nodded, but her gaze lingered. "Will you stay up?"

"Until the fire's settled." He hesitated. "Until I'm sure the house holds."

He didn't say the rest: Until I'm sure you do.

"Goodnight, Evan."

"Night, Lila."

He watched her climb the stairs, lantern light trailing her like a moving star. When she disappeared around the corner, he sat back down by the fire. The room felt both emptier and more alive than it had in years.

He picked up his sandpaper again, but his hands didn't move. Instead, he watched the fire pulse and thought about how storms ended—not all at once, but slowly, one quiet ember at a time.

And for the first time in a long while, he realized he wasn't waiting for it to be over.

He was waiting for her to come back downstairs, and the waiting itself felt like a mistake he was already rehearsing how to survive.

The wanting settled in his chest, steady and unwelcome, and he didn't know yet whether it was something that could be trusted.

Chapter 9

Lila told herself she was content to be alone.

The lie grew harder to maintain the longer the clock ticked above the mantel. She sat curled on the couch near the fire, wrapped in a quilt Ruth had left behind before retreating upstairs, her notebook resting open but forgotten in her lap.

Snow slanted sideways past the windows as dusk settled in, gusts so strong they made the panes shudder in their frames. Somewhere beyond the curtain of white, the world still existed—roads, towns, cell towers—but here in Midwinter, it might as well have been another planet.

Even Juniper had abandoned her for Walter's lap, leaving a faint indentation and a few stray hairs on the cushion beside her.

The quiet had been lovely at first but now it bordered on maddening. She needed something to do with her hands before her thoughts started pacing circles. Before she started reaching for a phone that couldn't save her from herself anyway.

Her eyes drifted toward the old cupboard in the corner of the room, stacked with mismatched mugs and a few dusty boxes tucked beneath. She slipped out from under the quilt and padded across the creaking floor. The first two boxes were labeled *Puzzles, Missing Pieces* and *Christmas Lights, Questionable.* The third, wedged behind a row of mugs, read *Board Games: Use at Your Own Risk.*

"Well," she muttered. "If that's not a challenge."

She dragged it out, sneezing as a puff of dust rose into the air. Inside were relics from another era: dominoes, checkers, a deck of cards with frayed corners, and a game of Scrabble whose box looked one snowstorm away from disintegration. She smiled, brushing off the cover.

"Scrabble it is."

The tiles rattled like ice in a glass as she carried the box to the low table near the fire. She set up the board, rediscovered the rules—mercifully written by Ruth on a napkin in loopy handwriting—and took a sip of tea that had gone lukewarm. She should have reheated it. She didn't. Lukewarm was honest.

She was sorting her tiles when Evan came down the stairs, the soft creak of his boots drawing her gaze. He wore a dark thermal shirt, sleeves pushed to his elbows, and had the look of someone who'd spent the day making sure the world stayed upright. His hair was still damp at the ends, probably from brushing off snow. The sight of his forearms should not have mattered. It did anyway.

"Ruth says the storm won't clear until tomorrow," he said. "You holding up okay?"

"Define okay."

He smiled faintly. "You look like you're plotting something."

"I found entertainment." She gestured toward the board. "Assuming this has all the letters."

He walked closer and studied the setup. "Scrabble."

"Don't sound so skeptical."

"I'm not. I just didn't take you for the word-game type."

"Why not?"

He pulled up a chair opposite her and sat down. "Because you use words for a living. I'd think that people in your line of work avoid them off-duty."

"Ah, so I'm predictable."

"Maybe."

"Then prove it. Play me."

He raised a brow. "You sure? I take board games seriously."

"So do I."

"You realize I grew up playing this during every power outage for twenty years."

She leaned in, eyes glinting. "Then you've had plenty of practice losing."

He laughed—an honest, warm sound that loosened something low in her chest. "All right, Ms. Moore. Don't say I didn't warn you."

The first few turns were polite—safe, simple words like *snow* and *lamp*. Soon the rhythm shifted. She played *quiet*;

he countered with *storm* that stretched across a triple word score.

"Oh, come on," she said.

"It's called strategy."

"It's called being smug."

"You're just mad because I'm winning."

She squinted at the board. "You're not winning by much."

"Yet."

Her next draw gave her letters that could go a dozen ways. She shifted them around, searching for something that fit without feeling like she was trying too hard. She finally placed *steady* to hook onto his *storm*.

Evan's gaze paused on the word. Not the board. The word. Then it lifted to her face. "Fitting," he said, and his voice stayed casual, but his eyes didn't.

"Don't patronize me."

"Wouldn't dream of it."

The storm rattled the windows, the howl of wind occasionally drowning out their laughter. Lantern light pooled between them, throwing gold across his face and highlighting the lines of concentration that appeared when he thought too hard about a move. She liked those lines. She hated that she liked them.

When he drew his next set of letters, she caught his brow furrow in frustration.

"Problem?"

"Too many vowels."

"Excuses already."

He smirked and spelled *alone*, stretching it from her *steady*.

Lila's fingers paused. The word lingered longer than it should have. *Alone*. The way she'd arrived here. The way she'd lived for too long. And the way she'd felt the second the pile-on started. Like she was standing in a crowded room and everyone had decided not to see her.

She cleared her throat. "Good one."

"Your turn."

She stared at her tiles, then added *home*, intersecting his *alone*.

Evan's gaze flicked up to meet hers. Something tightened in his expression, fast and unguarded. Not pity. Not sympathy. Like he didn't like the idea of her belonging to loneliness.

"Nice placement," he said.

"Thank you."

Silence settled—not awkward, just charged. The fire popped, throwing a warm glow across the board. Her heart thudded faster than she cared to admit.

He broke it first, voice low. "Guess you're catching up."

"Guess I am."

They played another round, the teasing easy, the laughter coming faster. At one point, Juniper jumped onto the table and sent half the tiles scattering.

Lila gasped. "Juniper! That's a twenty-point penalty!"

The cat blinked slowly, unimpressed, and sat squarely on *home*.

Evan laughed, bending to collect the tiles. "She's ruthless."

"She's your cat," Lila said, crouching to help. Their hands met under the table, fingers brushing. The contact sent a small spark up her arm—fleeting but impossible to ignore.

He stilled, looking at her. For half a second, his hand didn't move away either.

She pulled back first, pretending to focus on the board, but the air between them had changed. Warmer, alive.

"She does that on purpose," Evan said softly.

"What?"

"Makes sure nobody forgets she's here."

"Maybe she likes the attention."

"Don't we all."

The words hung between them—simple, true, heavier than they should've been. Lila swallowed. Because attention used to feel like oxygen—measured, tracked, counted. Now it felt like a fire she didn't trust.

Outside, the wind rose again, throwing snow in dense spirals past the window. The lodge creaked but held, built for weather like this.

When they finally tallied the score, Lila had lost by four points. She threw her hands up. "Unbelievable."

"A fair match," Evan said, clearly pleased with himself.

"You've been practicing for decades."

"And yet you nearly beat me."

She arched a brow. "Are you saying I'm a natural?"

"I'm saying you learn fast." His eyes held hers a beat too long. "And you don't quit."

The compliment landed in a place that wasn't ready. Lila's laugh came out a little too bright. "I hate losing."

"I noticed."

She started scooping tiles back into the pouch, just to do something with her hands. The pouch snagged on the edge of the table and spilled again.

"Perfect," she muttered, embarrassed by how sharp the moment hit. *Stupid. It's just tiles.*

Evan reached across the table, not for the tiles at first, but for her wrist. His grip was light, steady. Not stopping her. Grounding her. "Hey," he said quietly. "It's fine."

Her throat tightened. "I know."

But they both knew she wasn't talking about Scrabble.

He let go, slow. Like he didn't want to. Like he knew he shouldn't hold on.

The firelight danced between them—flicker, shadow, glow—and she felt something stir under her ribs that had nothing to do with cold.

"Rematch tomorrow?" she asked, breaking the moment before it became too real.

"Tomorrow," he agreed. "If the storm lets us."

"If not, I'll just keep practicing until I win."

"Spoken like someone who hates losing."

"I prefer the term strategically motivated."

He chuckled and leaned back. "You're trouble, Lila Moore."

"Good trouble, I hope."

"The jury's still out."

She smiled into her mug, heart doing something uncomfortably light. The wind howled outside, but inside the lodge it was all warmth and laughter—the kind that settled in your chest and refused to leave. The kind that made you forget what you were running from. Which was the most dangerous part.

When she finally went to bed, the storm still raged, but it didn't feel threatening anymore. It felt like part of the story—loud and wild on the outside, quiet and too hopeful on the inside.

For the first time in a long while, she wasn't counting the hours until the storm passed. She was counting the ways this could ruin her if she let herself want it.

And hating herself for wanting it anyway.

Chapter 10

The fire had burned down to its bones by the time Lila went upstairs. Evan sat where she'd been, the quilt still warm across the chair. Juniper had claimed the Scrabble board as a throne, tail flicking across the square where home intersected alone.

He stared at it longer than he meant to.

He smiled despite himself. The cat always knew where to sit.

He leaned forward, tracing the dents and scratches on the tabletop. Every storm night used to be the same—lantern light, soup on the stove, wind shaking the windows—but this one wasn't.

Her laughter had changed the shape of the place.

He still felt it in his chest, that easy, genuine sound that slipped past every layer of guarded calm he'd built. He wasn't used to thoughts that made him want to listen.

Worse, he wasn't used to missing them the moment they stopped.

He rose to check the fire, fed it another log, then paused. His body knew these motions by heart. It was the rest of him that felt unsettled, like something had shifted a few inches out of alignment and refused to slide back.

He glanced toward the stairs, where her lantern light had vanished earlier. She'd said goodnight with a smile that lingered. Not polite. Not careful. Present. He'd told himself not to think too hard about it.

Thinking too hard was a storm of its own.

He did his usual rounds: checked latches, windows, the kettle, listened for the hum of the generator. The work steadied him. It always had. When he reached the front door, he opened it on instinct. Cold air rushed in sharp and clean, cutting through the warmth clinging to his clothes.

He stepped out, boots sinking ankle-deep, and lifted his face into the wind.

Sometimes it felt good to let the cold have him for a minute. It reminded him he was still part of the world outside these walls. That he hadn't gone soft. That he hadn't forgotten how to stand alone.

Tonight, though, the silence inside felt louder than the wind.

He shut the door and locked it out of habit. Juniper was waiting on the stairs, yellow eyes gleaming in the firelight.

"Yeah," he said quietly. "I know."

She blinked. Judgmental. Accurate.

He crossed back to the fire and sank into the chair Lila had used. Her mug sat half-full on the table. He reached for it without thinking, thumb brushing the rim—then stopped.

Don't do that.

He set it down untouched. "Don't be an idiot," he muttered.

She wasn't staying. People like her never did. They arrived bright and curious, tried on quiet like a borrowed coat, then left when the weight of it got real. He'd seen it before. He'd lived it.

And yet—she'd asked about his life. Not the job. Not the weather. Him. She'd listened without pity. Smiled like she wasn't already halfway gone.

That was the dangerous part.

He banked the fire, dimmed the lanterns, and sat in the half-light watching snow blur the glass. His father used to say certain moments stuck to you like burrs—small, ordinary things that lodged deep and refused to let go.

This felt like one of those moments.

When he finally stood, knees cracking, he slowed outside her door. A thin line of lantern light glowed beneath it. She wasn't asleep yet.

He almost knocked.

Just to make sure she was warm.

Just to say goodnight again.

Just to hear her voice once more before the quiet swallowed it.

His hand hovered, then dropped.

That would cross a line he wasn't ready to redraw. Not when wanting her already felt like stepping onto ice without knowing how thick it was.

So he kept walking.

When he lay down, he left the door cracked—habit, he told himself. In case the storm worsened. In case something needed fixing.

But as he stared at the ceiling and listened to the wind press against the walls, he knew better.

He was listening for her footsteps.

And for the first time in years, the thought of being the only one awake didn't feel like peace.

It felt like loss waiting to happen.

Chapter 11

The sound started as nothing more than a snap.

A sharp pop from the hearth—ordinary, almost dismissible—until the air shifted and the scent of smoke turned acrid.

Lila looked up from her notebook just in time to see a spark leap from the open iron grate and land in the basket of kindling beside it. The dry wood flared fast, flames licking upward with alarming hunger.

"Evan!" she shouted, the sound tearing out of her before thought caught up.

He was there instantly, crossing the room in long strides. He hooked the burning pieces with the iron poker and kicked the basket clear, smoke rising in gray ribbons that swallowed the glow of the room.

"Move back," he said, voice low, unyielding.

She obeyed, pulse slamming hard enough to drown out reason. Evan grabbed a wool blanket, dropped to one knee, and smothered the flames with practiced precision.

The hiss was sharp.

Then gone.

Silence rushed in to fill the space where fire had lived seconds earlier. He nudged the grate shut and checked the stone beneath the hearth with the back of his hand, then nodded once.

Lila pressed a hand to her chest. Her heart felt too big for her ribs. Smoke lingered—bitter, heavy—but the danger had passed.

Evan coughed once, sweeping the air clear with his arm. "You okay?"

"I think so." She scanned the room, adrenaline still buzzing. "That could've gotten bad."

"It didn't." His eyes moved over the hearth, the floor, the room—inventory complete. Only then did the tension leave his shoulders. "You did the right thing. Calling out."

She tried for a joke. "Screaming your name is kind of my emergency protocol now."

That earned her a quick, crooked grin. "Effective."

"This happens in weather like this," he said. "Dry air. One spark. Doesn't mean you did anything wrong."

He carried the singed blanket to the door and opened it wide. Cold air rushed in, dragging smoke with it.

"Grab your coat," he said. "We need to clear this out."

She wrapped herself in the quilt instead, tugging it close like armor. Together, they propped open the doors, letting the wind cut through the lodge. Her hair whipped loose, the scent of scorched wood and pine clinging to her clothes.

"Midwinter's version of fresh air," she said, voice still unsteady.

"Not subtle," he agreed.

When the air finally cleared, he shut the doors and turned to her, his gaze searching her face. "You sure you're all right?"

She nodded, though the truth was more complicated. "Fine. Just shaken."

His brow furrowed. "You didn't do anything wrong."

"I did." She sank onto the couch, clutching the quilt tighter. "I left the grate open. I wasn't paying attention. I was somewhere else."

"Where?"

Not casual. Not procedural. Curious.

She swallowed. "Thinking about things," she said quietly.

He didn't interrupt.

"I told myself it was work—writing, documenting, staying relevant. But it became about being seen." Her voice wavered. "If I disappeared, I vanished. So I stopped disappearing." A brittle laugh escaped. "Turns out being everywhere all the time makes you invisible anyway."

Something in Evan's posture changed. Not movement—attention.

"I know how that feels," he said.

She looked up. "You?"

He nodded. "Different shape. Same damage." He dragged a hand through his hair. "I told you my fiancée left. I didn't tell you why."

"You don't have to—"

"I do." His breath left him slow. "We were supposed to marry the winter after my dad died. I thought building something solid here would fix what was breaking." His jaw tightened. "She wanted out. We fought. The night before she tried to leave, the road iced over five miles south of town. She was in the hospital for days. Long enough to give me hope. Then she was gone." He swallowed. "After that, people needed someone to blame."

Lila's chest constricted. "Evan..."

The fire popped, a small echo of what almost happened.

They sat in the quiet aftermath—storm whispering, embers glowing.

"I'm sorry," Lila said. "That kind of loss doesn't age. It just settles."

He met her gaze. Really met it. "And you?"

She didn't dodge this time. "I came here because I was tired of performing my life. I didn't know how to stop without disappearing completely."

Her voice softened. "And now I'm here—with you—and it feels like staying might cost something too."

That landed.

He didn't look away. "It does."

The honesty of it made her breath catch.

She reached for his hand—not thinking, not planning. Just needing contact. Her fingers brushed his, tentative.

He didn't pull back.

Instead, he turned his hand slowly, palm up, offering choice instead of claim.

She took it.

The warmth was immediate. Steady. Dangerous.

They stayed like that—storm outside easing into long sighs, smoke thinning, the lodge holding.

For the first time in a long while, Lila didn't feel like she was bracing for impact or escape. The way he held still with her, as if the moment itself mattered, made her aware of how fragile it all was.

The fire dimmed to embers. The quiet didn't empty. It asked something of her.

Chapter 12

The fire was mostly ash by the time Lila went upstairs, her quilt trailing behind her like a comet's tail. The smell of smoke still clung to the air—wood, wool, and something faintly sweet, like burned cinnamon.

Evan crouched at the hearth, stirring the last of the embers until they sighed into a faint red glow. The heat licked his knuckles, steady and real. He nudged a log that didn't need it, adjusted the damper that was already right.

Control felt safer than stillness.

He'd lived through more storms than he could count, but none that felt like this one. Usually there was relief when a crisis passed—satisfaction in fixing something that had threatened to break. Tonight, there was only a restless pulse behind his ribs that wouldn't ease.

When things mattered most, they didn't always fail slowly. Sometimes they gave way all at once. No warning. No chance to brace.

Her voice replayed in his head. *I stopped disappearing. Being everywhere made me invisible anyway.*

He knew that emptiness. He'd built a life around avoiding it—learning every system here by heart, checking and rechecking until his hands ached. People mistook it for peace.

It wasn't peace. It was camouflage.

He brushed soot from his palms. Juniper sat nearby, tail curled neatly around her paws, watching him with mild contempt.

"Yeah," he murmured. "Not my best fire."

The cat yawned.

"Don't start," he said, almost smiling.

He cracked a window. Cold air rushed in, cutting through the lingering warmth. Outside, the snow had softened into lazy flurries, the storm finally losing its grip. He watched longer than necessary, as if the weather might change its mind.

The quiet pressed in—not empty, not sharp. Waiting.

When he turned back, his gaze caught on the Lake Room window. Her lantern glowed faintly inside, soft and golden. The only light upstairs. A living thing in the dark.

She hadn't lied about why she came here. Her burnout wasn't performative. It was bone-deep. She'd built a life around connection, and it had stranded her anyway.

He understood that more than he liked.

People didn't expect silence to take everything from you. They expected noise to do the damage.

Her notebook lay open where she'd forgotten it, pencil tucked inside. As he reached to slide it away from the hearth, a single line caught the lantern light near the middle of the page.

The fire wasn't the only thing that burned tonight.

Something tight loosened in his chest. Not relief. Recognition.

"Poet," he murmured, and closed the notebook gently, as if it might bruise.

The air still held traces of her—cedar shampoo, smoke, tea leaves. Familiar already. Too familiar for a woman who wasn't supposed to matter this much.

It would have been easy to pretend this was temporary. Roads would clear. She would leave. He would go back to silence and systems and the safety of predictability.

But something had shifted tonight, and he didn't trust himself to pretend otherwise.

He'd told her about the night everything went wrong. Not details—just the shape of it. Snow. Motion. Then nothing holding where something should have been.

He hadn't spoken those words aloud in years.

This time, it hadn't felt like confession.

It had felt like risk.

"You're losing your edge," he muttered.

Juniper blinked slowly.

"Yeah," he said. "You warned me."

He made one last circuit of the lodge—latches, shutters, kettle, generator gauge. He checked the back door twice. The window latch again. Familiar sounds answered him from every corner. The building settling. Holding.

By the time he reached the stairs, the lantern upstairs had dimmed. The line of light beneath her door was gone.

He paused, one hand resting on the banister.

He could picture her there—hair loose, mind still turning, the quiet working its way into her bones. He didn't know what to call what lingered between them.

Not yet.

It was trust.

And trust was harder to undo.

He turned off the last lantern, leaving only the faint glow of dying coals. On his way up, he slowed outside her door. He rested his fingertips against the doorframe, then let them fall.

"Sleep well, Lila," he whispered.

The words felt like a promise he hadn't decided whether to keep.

In his room, the night was still. No wind. No storm. The kind of calm that followed danger and made you wonder what came next.

Evan lay back and stared at the ceiling beams, cataloging the lodge out of habit. Heat. Doors. Windows. Power.

All fine.

For once, his mind didn't drift to repairs or weather. It stayed with her—her hand in his when the flames died, the steadiness in her voice, the way she'd looked at him like staying might cost something and be worth it anyway.

He closed his eyes.

The storm had burned itself out.

But something else had just started to warm—and he wasn't sure he wanted to put it out.

Chapter 13

The storm was over, but morning hadn't quite forgiven the world yet.

Snow draped over the porch rail like a heavy quilt, soft and perfect, with no wind to disturb it. Trees stood frozen in the pale blue hush that follows a long night of chaos. The world looked rinsed clean—quiet to the point of reverence.

Lila blinked awake to the faint smell of smoke in her hair. Not a dream. The blanket on the chair by the hearth still showed the darkened edges where the fire had flared, the mark of something that had nearly gone wrong and hadn't.

She lay there for a moment, listening. No wind. No groan of beams. Just the low tick of cooling metal and the soft creak of the lodge settling into itself.

It was seven forty-three. Late by her old life. Early here.

She dressed slowly, choosing warmth over appearance, and padded downstairs in socks that slipped slightly on the worn wood. The lodge felt different in daylight—less mysterious, more honest. Still beautiful. Still holding.

In the kitchen, the air smelled like real coffee and wood smoke. Evan stood by the woodstove, flannel sleeves pushed to his elbows, hair damp and shoved back as if he'd washed up and not thought much past that. He handed her a mug without asking how she took it.

"Morning," he said.

"I'm on vacation," she answered when he teased her about sleeping in.

"From what?"

"Everything."

He smiled at that, small and understanding, like the word had weight he recognized.

Juniper announced herself, winding around his ankles in dramatic complaint until he passed Lila the scoop. Instant devotion. The cat ate like she'd invented hunger and was still offended no one had thanked her.

They ate muffins Ruth had left under a cloth, steam still trapped inside, the kind that crumbled softly instead of making a mess. Outside, the snow caught the light and threw it back through the windows, making the room glow as if lit from the floor up.

At the window, the lake was a white plate. Pines along the far shore stood like sentries, dark and patient.

"It doesn't feel real," Lila said. "Like we're inside a painting."

"Wait till the sun hits it," Evan said. "Everything turns gold."

She set her mug on the sill and opened her notebook. Lines came easy: window curves, roof slope, smoke curling from the chimney. She drew Evan leaning against the counter, half shadow, half light. She told herself it was practice. It looked like memory.

"You draw," he said, surprised and not.

"Sometimes."

"It's good."

"Careful," she said. "You'll ruin your reputation for rationed compliments."

He scratched the back of his neck. "I'll work on finding more."

The light broke through the clouds. The snow glittered. She drew without thinking about captions or posts or whether anyone would ever see it. Creating felt like breathing—necessary, unremarkable, lifesaving.

He watched from the doorway with his mug between his palms. The lodge had known functional quiet for a long time—the kind that kept things running. Her pencil made a softer kind, the kind a place leaned toward without knowing why.

"You make the lodge look different when you draw it," he said when she caught him watching.

"Different how?"

"Warmer."

Color rose to her cheeks that wasn't embarrassment. Being seen without judgment had weight. It made her want to stand still instead of performing something worth seeing.

He cleared his throat and set the mug down. "I'm going to check things outside before the sun gets slick. You want fresh air or more coffee?"

"Both. I'll help."

He almost said no, out of habit—the word already shaping itself in his mouth. Instead, he reached into the peg basket and held out a spare pair of wool socks.

"Boots first," he said. "Roof edge is icy."

Chapter 14

Outside, the cold bit clean. Their breath lifted in thin plumes that vanished almost as soon as they appeared. The porch steps were drifted to the first rail, the far corner of the railing sagging under the snow's weight like it had given up the argument overnight.

Lila paused at the top step, taking it in. The cold sharpened everything—the light, the sounds, even her thoughts. It felt honest out here. No filters. No soft edges.

"Start there?" she asked, nodding toward the steps.

"Start here," he said, handing her a push broom. "Sweep from the house out. Slow, so you don't pack it."

She nodded, testing the weight of the broom, then set to work. The bristles hissed against the wood. Evan's shovel followed a steady beat beside her—scrape, lift, toss. The rhythm settled quickly, the kind you fall into without talking.

The quiet carried small sounds: nails pinging faintly in the cold, the distant creak of trees shedding snow, the soft thud of powder hitting the ground. As the railing thawed, the smell of wet pine rose, clean and sharp.

"Tell me if I'm doing this wrong," she said, half serious.

"You'll know," he said. "The railing will complain."

"It already does," she said, pressing a little too hard.

He bit back a smile. "You're learning its language fast."

They freed the steps, then cleared a narrow path where the wind had carved a stubborn ridge. Snow slumped away in satisfying slabs, collapsing under its own weight.

"Your city-girl card might be revoked," he said.

"Recovering city girl," she said, breath fogging as she worked. "And I like work that shows."

He glanced at her then—not surprised, exactly, but impressed in a quiet way. She didn't rush. Didn't ask if she was doing enough. She just kept going, steady and present.

He tested the sagging corner post, then crouched to check the bracket, brushing snow from the metal with his glove. "Bracket loosened. We'll tighten it and add a brace."

"Translation?"

"Hold this," he said, passing her a short two-by. "And don't let me fall on my face."

She planted her boots, braced the wood, felt the vibration travel through her arms as he drove the screws home. The drill whined, then stopped. The railing rose a clean inch, solid and sure.

"That's it?" she said, eyes widening.

"That's it."

She ran her fingertips along the rail, feeling the difference immediately—the way it no longer shifted under pressure. "Satisfying."

"Most repairs are," he said. "They're honest. You put in the effort, they tell you right away if it worked."

They circled to the side path. Icicles hung from the roof edge, thick and glassy. Evan tapped them free with the shovel handle. They shattered on the packed snow like crystal bells.

"Beautiful," Lila said.

"Until they pull down the gutter."

"Less beautiful," she agreed.

At the generator shed, he brushed snow away and checked the lines with practiced hands. She watched him work—efficient, careful, unshowy. There was no hurry in him, just attention.

"You like fixing things," she said.

"I like knowing they'll hold when weather tests them."

She thought of last night's fire, the way he'd moved without panic. "They do," she said.

Back on the porch, he split a few logs. The axe landed clean, wood breaking open with a sharp crack. The scent of resin rose warm and sharp, cutting through the cold.

"Want to try?" he asked.

"I'll keep all my toes if it's all the same."

"Smart."

She swept the last of the powder from the doormat. The morning had warmed enough for snow to slide off the roof in slow sighs, thumping softly into the drifts below.

Inside, they stamped their boots and peeled off gloves. Heat wrapped around them immediately. Evan poured more coffee and slid a muffin toward her without comment.

"You did good out there," he said.

"Translation?" she asked.

"You didn't let me fall on my face."

"High bar," she said, smiling.

They stood at the counter, shoulders nearly touching, steam ghosting up between them. Through the window, the railing they'd fixed looked perfectly ordinary again—which was the point.

"Looks better," she said.

"Feels better," he said.

Their eyes met, a small, shared pride settling between them like a finished task—quiet, earned, and solid.

"Lunch after I check the roofline?" he asked.

"I'll make sandwiches," she said. "Bribery. Noted."

He nodded once, the corner of his mouth tipping up. "Deal."

Outside, sunlight slid across the lake and turned the white to gold. Inside, the ordinary morning held—and for once, ordinary felt like enough, which meant he was already imagining how it would end.

Chapter 15

The sun had found its confidence again. It spilled through the snow-covered trees in soft gold bands, glinting off drifts so bright Lila had to squint just to look at them. The whole world seemed to glitter, every branch wrapped in crystal, as if the storm had decided to leave something behind instead of just damage.

"Come on," Evan called over his shoulder. "You'll want to see it before the light changes."

Lila adjusted the borrowed scarf around her neck and followed him down the lodge steps. The snow squeaked beneath her boots, crisp and deep. Each breath came out in a puff of white. "You said we were just clearing the path," she said, half teasing, half winded.

"We are," he said, glancing back with a smile. "But it'd be a crime to stay inside on a morning like this."

The air felt alive—cold enough to sting but full of promise, the kind that made her lungs feel new. He hand-

ed her a snow shovel, old but sturdy, and pointed to the
narrow walkway leading toward the woodshed.

They worked quietly, the rhythm of shovel and
breath filling the space where words might have gone.
The work warmed her faster than she expected. When
they reached the end of the path, she leaned on the
shovel and looked up. The sun had climbed higher now,
setting the snow to shimmer like powdered glass.

"It's like the world's been reset," she said. "Everything clean again."

He paused, shovel resting against his shoulder.
"That's the best part of winter. It hides what's broken
for a while."

The words landed heavier than he probably meant
them to. She felt them settle in her chest. Instead of
asking, she said, "Show me the lake."

He hesitated—just a beat—then nodded. "Watch
your step. It's slick."

They moved through the trees, snow brushing their
coats, branches bowing under the weight of ice. The
trail opened suddenly, and the lake stretched out before them—frozen, vast, and impossibly still. Its surface
gleamed like glass, reflecting sky and mountain until the
horizon blurred.

Lila stopped short. "It's beautiful."

Evan came up beside her, close enough that she
felt his warmth through their coats. "Frozen since before Christmas. Some winters you can hear it groan at
night—the ice expanding."

"That sounds eerie."

"It's honest," he said. "Everything shifts. You just have to trust it'll hold."

She stared out over the wide white expanse, her pulse slowing, her thoughts thinning. She didn't realize she was smiling until he said, "You look lighter."

"Lighter?"

"Like you finally set something down."

"Maybe I did," she said.

He stepped onto the lake first, careful, deliberate. The ice groaned low and deep, a sound that vibrated up through her boots even from shore.

He turned back to her. "You coming?"

Her stomach fluttered. "I'm not exactly graceful on solid ground."

He held out his gloved hand. "Then it's a good thing I'm here."

She hesitated—just long enough to feel the fear, acknowledge it—then took his hand. It was warm, steady. When her boot slid, she gasped, fingers tightening instinctively in his grip.

"Easy," he murmured. "You're fine."

They stood together on the ice, breath mingling, the lake murmuring beneath them.

"You trust this?" she asked. Trust wasn't her strength these days, but if he could, she would try.

"The ice?"

"Not just the ice."

The wind skimmed across the lake, thin and restless. Evan didn't rush his answer.

"I lost my fiancé," he said quietly. "After that, I came here. I know this lake well enough to trust where it holds."

Lila nodded once. She didn't fill the silence. She stayed.

"All of it," he added.

Her fingers curled more firmly around his. "Trust takes time."

He met her gaze. "But you start somewhere."

They walked along the edge of the lake, slow and cautious, hands still joined. When she stumbled again, he caught her easily, his arm secure at her waist.

"See?" he said. "Balance is easier when you're not doing it alone."

She laughed, breathless, and the sound carried across the frozen water.

When they finally turned back toward the lodge, the path behind them was already softening under new snow.

It didn't matter.

Some moments weren't meant to last. They were meant to stay.

Chapter 16

By the time Evan and Lila reached the lodge again, the light had shifted—thinner now, the sun already angling toward afternoon. They'd made the decision quietly, the kind that didn't need discussion: a supply run while the road was open, before the weather changed its mind again.

Town had been efficient and impersonal. In and out. Bags loaded. No lingering.

Now the place looked the same as it had that morning. Smoke curled politely from the chimney. Snow rested clean and untouched along the rail they'd fixed together.

Lila stayed in the truck for a moment after Evan cut the engine.

The silence pressed in. Not the gentle quiet of the fire or the lake, but something tighter. Watchful.

"I should help Ruth unload," she said, reaching for the door handle.

"I've got it," Evan said, already stepping out.

She hesitated, then followed anyway. Inside, Ruth greeted them with a smile that dimmed a little when she took in their faces.

"Everything all right?" she asked, light but perceptive.

"Roads are fine," Evan said. He set the bags on the counter and started sorting without being asked. Flour here. Milk there. Efficient. Controlled.

Lila hung her coat and stood by the window, suddenly unsure where to put herself.

Ruth watched the exchange for another beat, then said, "Walter and I are heading upstairs for a nap. Storms wear him out." She squeezed Lila's arm gently as she passed. "You're always welcome here."

The words landed harder than they should have.

When they were alone again, Evan finished unloading and wiped his hands on a towel that didn't need it.

"I didn't know," he said finally. Not accusing. Just honest.

"I wasn't hiding it," Lila said. "I just... didn't bring it with me."

He nodded, but his jaw stayed tight. "I get wanting quiet. I just didn't like feeling blindsided."

That stung because it was fair.

She crossed her arms, not defensively—bracing. "I didn't want it to be the first thing you knew about me."

"And now it is," he said quietly.

She swallowed. "Is it?"

He looked at her then. Really looked. The way he had on the ice. "It doesn't change who you are. It changes how people act. And that matters here."

She exhaled, slow and shaky. "That's what I'm afraid of."

The lodge creaked softly around them, settling. The fire popped. Ordinary sounds. Still holding.

"I don't want this place to turn into content," she said. "Or me. Or us." The last word surprised her, but she didn't take it back.

Evan leaned against the counter, arms crossed now too. Not shutting her out. Grounding himself. "Then don't let it," he said. "But you have to decide what you're running from and what you're staying for."

She closed her eyes. Just for a second.

"I don't know yet," she admitted. "And that scares me."

He nodded. "Yeah. Me too."

The honesty sat between them, heavy but clean.

Outside, a truck passed on the reopened road, tires crunching, sound carrying farther than it should have. Proof that the world was moving again.

Lila turned toward the window. "I think I need some time. Not away from here. Just... quieter. Inside."

Evan didn't argue. That was the gift. "I'll check the roofline," he said. "Take the long way."

She smiled faintly. "Thank you."

As he pulled on his coat, he paused. "For what it's worth," he added, "I still like who you are when it's just us and the fire and the work that needs doing."

Her throat tightened. "Same."

He nodded once and stepped outside, the door closing softly behind him.

Lila stayed where she was, watching the snow drift from the pines. The lodge still held. The warmth hadn't vanished. But something had shifted—just enough to remind her that staying meant choosing, not hiding.

And for the first time, she understood that love didn't grow best in silence alone.

It grew where truth was allowed to be loud.

Chapter 17

The day began before the light did. She woke to the quiet kind of darkness that holds its breath. No storm. No generator. Only timber settling and the faint brush of branches along the eaves. Somewhere above the lake a bird tried one note, thought better of it, and stopped.

Lila lay still, counting heartbeats until the room and her body separated. Quilt. Wool blanket. Smoke in her hair. The window eased from graphite to pearl, the lodge exhaled, and so did she.

On paper she'd always been a morning person. Up before dawn. First post at seven. Inbox sorted by eight. The habit had been useful and hollow. Here, morning arrived with no applause. No metrics. Just a room brightening because the sun found it.

She dressed in layers and tucked a pencil behind her ear without thinking. At the door she doubled back for the small leather notebook on the nightstand. Scuffed corners. Thread caught in the spine. It felt like a pocket that belonged to her.

The hall held a cool hush. The staircase gave two familiar creaks and delivered her to lantern light and the steady breath of the woodstove. Juniper stretched on the rug, then trotted over like she had waited years.

"Morning," Lila whispered, rubbing the cat's jaw. Purr. Approval granted.

Ruth cut biscuit dough with a drinking glass. Flour dusted her cardigan. The room smelled of butter and a bright curl of citrus. "You're early," Ruth said. "First batch in five."

"My stomach woke up first. Can I help?"

"Kettle," Ruth said. "Evan stole the good coffee for the porch. We'll pretend loose-leaf tea is exciting."

"Blasphemy," Lila said, smiling as she set the kettle on. Her hands felt both restless and content, like a dog off the leash that decided to heel anyway.

"Walter still sleeping?" she asked.

"Like a saint," Ruth said. "He spent last night lecturing the lamp for flickering. Exhausting work."

Lila laughed and glanced at the windows. The porch wore a clean white shoulder. The lake lay smooth and sure. If she'd been her old self, she would have reached for a phone to frame it. The reflex rose and fell.

"Eat before you disappear into your head," Ruth said, gentle. "Apricot jam. The good one."

"There's a bad one?"

"Yes," Ruth said without blinking. "We do not speak of it."

Lila ate a biscuit hot enough to sting, then wrapped her fingers around a steaming mug. Ruth slid another tray into the oven and hummed. Juniper chirped like she recognized the song and padded away on secret business.

"I'm going to write," Lila said.

"Write for yourself first," Ruth said. "Then decide if the rest deserve it."

The words landed and stayed. "Yes, ma'am."

The desk by the Lake Room window belonged to another century. Narrow drawer. Clean top scarred by faint rings and one old burn. She found ivory stationery and a worn fountain pen, then set both aside for her own pen. The window gave her pines bowed with snow, the path Evan had cleared, the shed roof capped in frost, the lake holding steady.

She touched a clean page.

What do I want from life?

The question sat there like a stranger she might feed into friendship. Her throat tightened. She wrote it again to give the first line company.

What do I want from life? Not the public answer. The true one.

The kettle hissed and settled. The room smelled of jam and wood flame with a thin braid of cold air under the door. Her neck loosened, and the pencil moved.

I want mornings without rushing. I want to stop measuring myself in squares and seconds. I want to belong to the day I'm in.

Another breath.

I want work that feels like a hand under water finding another hand. I want to be useful without disappearing.

Her eyes burned. She let them. The words didn't need to be pretty, only honest enough to make her flinch.

She wrote about a surface that looked like glass and held like faith. About the fire finding breath when Evan moved the poker and the room answering. She didn't write his name.

I want to be seen without performing. I want to learn the shape of quiet and not fear it means I've been forgotten.

From the kitchen came plate clinks and Walter's voice, cheerful and sleep-rough, followed by Ruth's fond cluck. The lodge kept what mattered and let the rest slide off the roof.

I want the courage to leave the wrong room. I want to learn to keep a fire steady. I want to learn to stay.

Stay. Small word. Heavy.

There were easier answers. Money. A trip. A new lens. She had wanted all of that and sometimes still did. But the wanting had shifted. Here, biscuits and a swept path made the day count.

She wrote one last line.

I want to belong to myself in a way that lets me belong to a place and maybe a person without disappearing into either.

She boxed the maybe. She folded the page and slid it into the drawer beneath the stationery. The drawer closed with a friendly sound. Secret kept.

Juniper appeared on the sill to supervise.

"Keep my secrets," Lila said.

The cat blinked slow.

Lila sketched. The leaning porch lantern. The round of snow softening the roof. The shed's honest crooked corner. A small figure near the shed came into being before she named him.

A floorboard creaked. Evan stood in the wide doorway with a mug and a shallow, borrowed-looking smile.

"Morning," he said, voice low to match the room. "You beat the sun."

"Tea and greed for biscuits. Your excuse?"

"Habit. Checking windows twice."

"Any rebellion?"

"The Lake Room latch is sulking," he said, nodding to the glass. "I'll tighten it after breakfast."

"You caught it before the wind did. Gold star."

"Careful," he said. "I'll get spoiled."

He stood to the side and took in the sketch from a respectful distance. "You got the roof line right."

"I gave the lantern dignity," she said. "It may not deserve it in daylight."

"It tries," he said. "Everything does."

"Ruth says biscuits are ready."

"Walter will swear he wants one and eat five," Evan said, setting the mug down. "I'll stay out of the jam debate."

"Coward."

"Survivor," he said, smile settling. "You okay this morning?"

"Better than I used to be," she said.

He nodded, as if she'd given a weather report he trusted. "Good."

He left, and the doorway felt warm for a beat before returning to itself. Lila tucked the sketchbook under the blotter, then let the morning pull her toward the kitchen.

Breakfast moved like grace. Ruth guarded tongues from burns. Walter told a story about a snowplow made of bacon. Evan fixed the back-door latch between bites. Lila dried plates with attention usually saved for lenses. Warmth crept up her forearms and stayed.

At the sink, Evan thumbed the window latch. The thin metal chatter went still after a quarter turn and another eighth. "Cooperative," he said.

"Teach me that trick."

"Pay attention. Go slow. Stop when it feels right."

That belonged to more than windows. She let it hang.

Ruth shooed them out with a towel. "Go make yourself useful elsewhere. I have a date with 1973."

Walter saluted and kissed her cheek. Lila felt the good ache of watching a simple thing that wasn't simple at all.

She drifted back to the Lake Room to tuck the notebook deeper. The folded page had crept forward. She eased it back and set a flat gray stone with a white stripe atop the stack. A quiet horizon. She rested her palm there a second longer than needed.

At the lobby window, sunlight pulled a sheen from the lake. Evan crossed the porch with a coil of cord, glanced in, and lifted two fingers. I see you, without a spectacle. She raised her mug. Answer given.

Back at the desk she made an inventory, not a confession.

Today I didn't reach for my phone when the light changed.

Today I wrote for myself and the room didn't collapse.

Today I want to keep steady things that are not fires or windows.

She dated the page and slid it under the blotter so the edge peeked, a breadcrumb for later. The room felt larger when she stood, not because the walls moved, but because she had.

"Keep," she told the day at the threshold. "Just keep."

The porch glittered in a small wind. The kettle sighed and settled. Her pulse matched it without being asked.

For the first time in a long while, she didn't feel watched. She felt held. By a place. By a version of herself she wanted to keep.

Chapter 18

The day held a clean-edged quiet he liked best. No wind bullying the eaves. No generator chewing at the air. Beams settling. Radiators ticking. The kettle's satisfied breath.

He tightened the back-door latch and wiped his hands. Ruth hummed to a seventies playlist and kept Walter from negotiating with hot biscuits. Juniper patrolled like a small tyrant.

"Guest-room windows before lunch," Ruth said.

"On it," he said.

The Lake Room drew him first. He knocked once and eased the door. Empty. Bed made. Desk neat. Sun pooling on the surface like a small lake.

The window latch chattered a complaint. "Sulking," he said, setting down his screwdriver.

A slip of paper peeked from under the blotter. He told himself to leave it. Heat from the radiator curled the edge out a fraction more.

"All right," he muttered, sliding it back. His eyes caught a line he didn't intend to read.

Today I didn't reach for my phone when the light changed.

He could have stopped.

Today I wrote for myself and the room didn't collapse.

Something eased in his chest. He pushed the page back and stood as if the wood had slapped his hand. He hated trespassing. The lines stayed.

He tightened the latch. Quarter turn. Test. Another eighth. The chatter went quiet. The sash settled with a clean click.

A flat stone sat on the stationery stack. Gray with a white stripe. A seam that held while the rest shifted. He touched it with a knuckle and left it.

Footsteps on the stairs. He stepped back from the window and picked up the screwdriver like a man with an alibi.

Lila stood in the doorway with a mug, hair already escaping the knot. "Caught you," she said, amused.

"Window," he said, tapping the latch. "It was complaining."

"Not anymore," she said, testing it. "That's weirdly satisfying."

"Better than coffee," he said before he could stop himself.

Her mouth curved. Warmth moved through his ribs, and he found the lock keeper fascinating.

"Ruth sent me up to make sure you're not skipping lunch," she said.

"I'll be down," he said. "She threatened jam."

"Apricot? The good one?"

"Did she tell you about the bad one?"

"She says we don't talk about the bad one," she said, conspiratorial. She set her mug on the desk. He looked anywhere but the blotter. The screws didn't look back.

"It's different in here in the morning," she said, watching the square of sun. "The room minds its business. You mind yours."

"That's how a house stands," he said. "Every part does its job. No fuss."

"Do you ever ask for applause?" she asked lightly, curiosity under it.

"Not my style," he said, clicking the latch one last time. "Thank you," she said.

"For the latch?"

"For looking after things." A beat. "And people."

He nodded, grateful for a tool that didn't require feelings to work. "Lunch."

She took a step, then paused. "You don't have to carry everything alone just because you can."

He could have deflected. Instead, maybe because of two lines under a blotter, he said, "I know."

They went down together. Soup. Small gears of conversation. Walter's fish story that grew a surname. Ruth refilled bowls like a sacrament. Lila laughed at a mediocre joke and made it better. When she laughed, something in her shoulders unknotted.

He made his rounds and came back to return the screw-driver to the bits drawer. The slip of white still showed a hair under the blotter. He didn't touch it. He didn't need to. The words had done their work.

In the lobby she dried plates with sleeves pushed up. Juniper supervised like a firm union. "Windows are good," he said. "So is Ruth's playlist," she said.

"Don't insult my taste," Ruth called from the kitchen. "Your generation didn't invent joy."

"Wouldn't dare," Lila said.

They drifted toward the foyer without deciding to. At the door she tugged on boots.

"Walk?"

"Cold."

"I have layers and a stubborn streak."

"Fair," he said, holding the door as the cold pushed in.

They stepped out together, the porch boards snapping softly beneath their boots, breath turning visible as the quiet closed around them.

They checked the shed. He touched the generator hous-ing and listened. She waited without filling the quiet.

On the way back she said, "I wrote this morning. For me."

"Good."

"Felt strange. Good-strange. Like talking to someone I used to be."

"Keep going."

"I think I will."

At the porch she brushed snow from the rail. "Can I ask something that might be weird?"

He became suddenly aware of how close she stood, of the shared heat neither of them mentioned.

"Try me."

"If you saw words of mine by accident, what would you do?"

The rope between them drew tight. He didn't lie. "Put them back. Pretend I didn't, unless the truth would keep you from getting hurt."

She studied him. "I appreciate that."

He swallowed. Honesty had sanded him down. "I saw a corner," he said. "Under your blotter. I read a line I shouldn't have. I'm sorry." He waited for disappointment, for the careful distance people took when trust cracked. It didn't come, and that unsettled him more than anger would have.

"Which line?"

"About the room not collapsing."

Relief flickered in her eyes. "That one can be public. The rest... not yet."

"They're yours."

"Thank you," she said, no edge. "For telling me."

"Didn't feel right to carry it alone."

"That makes two of us," she said.

Cold found skin where wool ended. He felt a new rhythm settling, not a rush and not a retreat. A careful step closer with respect.

She took the stone from her pocket and showed the white stripe. "I've been using it to keep pages still."

"Quartz seam," he said. "A line that held when the rest shifted."

"Feels like a metaphor."

"Everything does if Ruth gets a hand in it," he said.

She laughed, bright in the cold.

Inside, they shed hats and steam lifted from their hair. At the desk she set the stone back on the stack and pressed her palm there for a heartbeat.

"I'm going to keep writing," she said. "If you hear the scratch and think I'm working, don't worry. It's just me."

"The house likes healthy noises," he said, embarrassed and earnest all at once. "Kettle. Good fire. Pencil on paper belongs."

"I'll try to give it more of that."

He stepped back and let the room belong to her again. At the threshold he paused. "Lila."

She looked up.

"Your room won't collapse," he said. He meant more than the room.

"I know," she said. "You fixed the latch."

In the hall he pressed his palm to the wall the way he always did, listening. The lodge felt steadier. Not because of the screws he turned. Because of the sound of a pencil in a room that didn't demand proof.

Downstairs, Ruth's song changed and Walter hummed half a beat behind. Juniper trotted past like she planned to issue notes. Evan pulled on his coat and stepped into the bright cold to check the shed once more before dusk.

He didn't need to. Everything was holding.

He went anyway. Some routines you keep because they make sense. Some because the world has started to feel like it might again, and you want to hear it settle.

Chapter 19

The drip woke Lila before the light did.

Not loud. Not dramatic. Just a slow, steady tap on the braided rug beside the bed. She lay there, half awake, listening to the rhythm until she could predict the next drop. She counted three before her body decided it was done pretending to sleep. The rest of Ember Lodge stayed hushed, the kind of stillness that made every sound—creaking floorboard, whispering wind—feel amplified. The air smelled faintly of pine smoke and wool.

She pushed the blankets back and slid her feet into thick socks. The windowpane glowed pale blue, the light of early morning after a heavy snow. Outside, the world was blanketed in silence—pines bowing under their burden, the lake beyond caught in a sheet of dull pewter. When she leaned close, she spotted a dark oval in the snow just below the eave. The roof had taken on more than it could handle. A thin vein of icicles notched the edge above her window, clear and sharp. Tiny, but they always grew fast when the day decided to thaw.

A drop landed squarely on the rug.

She sighed, picked up the ceramic mug she'd been using as a makeshift vase, plucked out the cedar sprig, and set the mug beneath the leak. She glanced at the tiny ceiling crack the water had traced. Hairline now. The kind that pretends to behave until a warm afternoon arrives.

Footsteps creaked in the hallway.

She recognized them instantly—Evan's easy, deliberate stride. The sound settled something in her chest before she'd decided it should. She opened the door before he could knock.

"Morning," he said, voice rough from sleep. The brim of his knit cap had left a faint crease on his forehead, and his breath clouded the cold air between them. He carried a toolbox in one hand and a coil of radio cord in the other. "Ruth heard you moving around. Said you were probably counting drips by now."

"I was," Lila said. "I was winning, too."

He stepped past her and looked toward the ceiling. His gaze took in the mug, the rug, the thin crack the water had traced along the plaster. He cataloged it the way he did everything—quietly, thoroughly, like it mattered. "Ice dam or a bad seam vent," he murmured. "I'll check it."

"*We'll* check it," she said.

His brows lifted. "You're planning to help patch a roof in January?"

"I'm planning to hold the ladder, hand you things, and be useful."

"Useful's a relative term."

"Useful means not letting you do everything yourself," she countered. "Besides, I want to learn."

He studied her for a moment, longer than the question required, as if deciding whether this was about the roof or something else entirely. "Fine," he said finally. "But we do it by the book. Crampons, harness, tie-off, second line from the chimney bracket. No cowboy moves."

"I don't own cowboy boots," she said lightly. "But I do have persistence and no shame, so if I fall, at least I'll look committed."

His mouth curved, faint but real. The look warmed something low and unexpected in her ribs. "Gloves, warm layers, and if you can find the spare cleats, you can keep me from sliding off your nice view."

While he fetched the ladder and gear, Lila layered up—thermals, jeans, sweater, borrowed parka, hat pulled low. She caught sight of herself in the mirror and decided the crooked angle of the hat suited her mood: determined, slightly ridiculous. Braver than yesterday. As she passed the small dome camera at the end of the hall, its tiny status light blinked once, an innocent reminder that up here even the quiet sometimes had witnesses. She didn't like the idea of being seen again, and that struck her.

Downstairs, the great room smelled of woodsmoke and coffee. Walter sat at the table with the morning paper, humming off-key. "Roof walk this morning?" he asked.

"There's a leak in room three."

"Ah, south eave." He pointed his spoon toward the ceiling. "Tell Evan to anchor off the chimney bracket.

Ridgepole creaks like my back. And if the sun comes out strong, you'll hear the ice run like a herd. Folks mistake it for thunder."

Evan returned through the side door, bringing a gust of cold with him. He set the ladder near the mudroom and handed her a pair of cleats.

"For your boots," he said.

"How do you know they'll fit?"

"Because I keep spares that fit most feet. I like when people stay upright."

They pulled on coats and stepped back out together. The cold hit them like a baptism. Their breath fogged in front of them as they crossed the deck. The world shimmered blue with early light.

Evan strapped the ladder to the porch rail, checked the anchor line twice, and clipped his harness.

"Belt and suspenders?" she asked.

"Belt, suspenders, and a partner who won't let go." His eyes flicked to hers. "That's you."

"Happy to be your suspenders."

He shook his head, the hint of a smile warming his expression. "Don't make me laugh on frozen wood."

Lila braced herself at the ladder's base while he climbed, steady and deliberate. He crawled along the roofline on his stomach, spreading his weight. From below, she could hear the scrape of his tool against ice, the soft thud of loosened snow. Every few minutes, he brushed snow aside, sending glittering sheets cascading past her boots. Above her, the icicle fringe chimed a thin warning as the light strengthened.

"You were right," he called down. "Ice dam. Water's backing up over the flashing."

"I love being right," she said.

He laughed—a quick, low sound that vibrated somewhere inside her chest. She felt it there longer than she expected. "Send up the scraper."

She clipped the flat scraper to the line and watched it rise toward him. He worked methodically, clearing the dam, sprinkling pet-safe de-icer, scraping again. The sun began to crest the ridge, light catching the frozen lake below. It was beautiful in that sharp, unrepeatable way—temporary and quiet. Beauty here always came with conditions.

When he reached the section above her window, she could hear him humming under his breath. The sound carried through the cold air like a secret meant only for her. He asked for the patch kit next, and she climbed a few rungs to pass it up.

He pried a shingle edge and swore softly.

"Problem?"

"Just a lifted seam. I'll tack it and seal it for now." A pause. "We'll need a proper repair when the thaw hits. South eave never forgets a weak winter."

"It feels like we're living in a snow globe," she said, watching the flakes swirl from his movements.

He chuckled. "Are there marshmallows in this metaphor?"

"Always."

She smiled up at him, and the quiet between them felt companionable—safe—until the hammer slipped.

It happened in an instant. The handle grazed his exposed wrist above the glove, and she heard the dull smack before she saw the red line bloom against his skin.

"Evan!"

"I'm fine," he said automatically, but his tone betrayed the sting. His balance never slipped but he did grunt loudly.

"Come down."

"I can finish—"

"Come down."

The command surprised her as much as it did him. He secured the hammer, crawled carefully back to the ladder, and descended. She stayed close, ready to steady him if he slipped, her heart thudding hard against her ribs. A brittle pop echoed along the ridge as a strip of ice let go somewhere above, the kind of harmless sound that still made you think about weight and what happened when it shifted.

When he stepped onto the deck, she took his arm without thinking. "Let me see."

The cut wasn't deep, but it was ugly—a scraped line already darkening around the edges. He brushed it off, but she wasn't having it. "Inside," she said. "Now."

They left the ladder where it was and headed through the mudroom. The warmth inside hit her face like sunlight. Walter rose from his chair the second he saw the blood.

"First aid kit's under the coffee station," he said, already moving aside. "And tell Ruth not to worry about the camera. It records over itself every forty-eight hours."

Evan didn't protest as she guided him to the sink. The warm water ran pink for a few seconds before clearing. He hissed when she dabbed the cut, closing his eyes.

"Okay?" she asked.

He gave a low hum that might have been yes.

"That sounded like an 'I'm pretending I'm fine' noise," she said.

He cracked one eye open. "It's a 'you're doing fine' noise."

She smiled, relieved despite herself. He smelled faintly of cold air and cedar, and now of her cinnamon coffee where she'd spilled some on his sleeve. His pulse beat steady beneath her fingers as she worked. The steadiness grounded her more than she expected.

She blew lightly on the wound to cool it, then blushed at the childish instinct. He didn't move away. His gaze stayed on her face—steady, quiet, intent.

"You're good at this," he said softly.

"I've had practice patching up my own dumb mistakes," she said. "And I took a wilderness first aid course once. Mostly it taught me not to do things like this."

"Noted."

She applied butterfly strips across the scrape, her fingers brushing the fine hair on his forearm. When she looked up, he was already watching her. The fire behind him glowed low and amber, catching in the edges of his hair.

"Thank you," he murmured.

"You're welcome."

The kitchen had gone still except for the quiet tick of the fire. Juniper jumped onto a chair and circled once before curling into a ball. Walter retreated to his crossword, politely pretending not to notice the tension in the room.

"Do we finish the patch?" she asked finally.

"In a minute," he said. "The worst of the ice is melting. The leak should stop for now."

"Then we have a minute."

He was still close, his hand warm in hers. Neither of them seemed in a hurry to step back. The space between them felt fragile but certain, like something newly built that would hold if treated gently.

"Lila," he said quietly. Her name in his voice landed soft and deliberate.

"Yeah?"

"I keep trying to be careful about this," he said. "About you. About the way it feels when you walk into a room and everything shifts."

Her pulse jumped. The honesty startled her more than the closeness. "Careful's good," she said. "But maybe we can be honest while we're careful."

His eyes flicked to her mouth, then back again. He stepped a little closer, raising his uninjured hand to her cheek. The back of his fingers brushed her skin, tentative and warm.

The air thickened between them, firelight and breath and something that felt like the beginning of yes. She tilted her face up, close enough to feel his breath, when—

"Evan, darling, you on channel two?"

Ruth's voice burst from the battery-operated radio on the counter, clear and bright. "We've got a delivery question at the Outpost. Bennie says the plow drifted a ridge across the drive. If you're not in the middle of keeping our roof on, could you pop over?"

They both froze. The moment held for a beat before breaking into a shared, helpless laugh.

Evan pressed the button on the radio. "Copy, Ruth. On my way."

"Thank you, honey. And check the south eave drip when you have a second," Ruth added. "Our guest in room three is patient, but I don't want to test her goodwill with a wet rug."

Lila reached over and turned off the radio before it could say more. Their hands brushed. Neither pulled away immediately.

"I'll go help Bennie," he said. "Then come back and finish the patch. You shouldn't have any more leaks."

"Okay."

He hesitated, then set his hand lightly on her forearm. Not a hold, just contact. A promise without words. "You all right?"

She nodded. "I am."

He studied her a second longer, then nodded once and headed for the door. When it closed behind him, the kitchen felt bigger, softer. The mug under the drip upstairs waited, but the steady sound of water had already stopped.

Outside, sunlight broke across the snow. Inside, Lila stood very still, her pulse slow but sure, and wondered when careful had started to feel a lot like hope.

Chapter 20

The snow squeaked under Evan's boots, sharp and clean in the brittle morning air.

He walked the narrow path toward the Outpost Store, shoulders hunched against the cold, his breath trailing in pale ribbons. The radio sat clipped to his jacket, quiet now except for the occasional burst of static. He'd left the lodge only minutes ago, but his pulse still hadn't found its old, steady place.

He couldn't stop replaying it.

Not the near-kiss. Not the interruption.

The part before that, when she'd taken his wrist like it mattered where he hurt. The way she'd looked at him, not like a man who fixed things, but like a man who could be hurt and still be worth care. She hadn't filled the space with pity. She'd stayed in it until it felt like something you could stand on.

He exhaled, fog clouding in front of him. "Careful," he muttered. He'd said that word to her, but it was more for him than for her. Careful didn't stop ice from breaking. It only taught you which step would cost you the most.

The Outpost came into view around the curve, a squat log building half-buried in a snowbank. Bennie Riley stood outside with a shovel, waving like Evan was a rescue team instead of a man with a tool belt and a radio.

"Morning, son!" Bennie called. "You're a sight for sore eyes. Plow shoved half the ridge right up against my drive. Mae's been threatening to hitch the dog to a sled."

Evan gave a small grin. "Morning, Bennie. Let's keep Mae off sled duty. She'll make the dog unionize."

Bennie's laugh boomed across the white. Together, they started digging the plow ridge clear. The snow was dense and wind-packed, heavy enough to argue with every scoop. Evan fell into rhythm the way he always did. Shovel. Lift. Toss. Work made sense when feelings didn't.

But even as his arms warmed, Lila stayed in the back of his mind like a hand pressed to his chest.

He'd spent years convincing himself solitude was safety. Easier not to want. Easier not to hope. Easier to keep company with wood and pipes and seams that could be sealed if you did it right. But lately, every time she spoke, every time her laugh rang down the hall, something inside him uncoiled.

And it wasn't just attraction. It was recognition. The way she seemed to understand the quiet wasn't a preference so much as a shelter he'd built after the wrong winter.

Bennie leaned on his shovel, breathing hard. "Appreciate the help. Mae'll have cocoa waiting for you. You still taking your coffee black, or has that new lady at the lodge converted you?"

Evan's shovel slowed. "What new lady?"

Bennie's grin turned broad, delighted. "Don't play coy. Ruth said she's renting a room. The blogger girl. Mae says she's too pretty to be up here alone."

Something in Evan tightened, quick and hot. He hated how immediate it was, how instinctive.

"She's not up here for company," Evan said, too sharp.

Bennie's brows rose like he'd just found the thread he wanted to pull. "Maybe not," he said mildly, "but company seems to find folks whether they invite it or not."

Evan kept digging, harder now, the shovel blade biting into the ridge with more force than needed.

Bennie nodded toward the Outpost window, where a flyer was taped crooked: *MIDWINTER THAW SALE, LAST WEEK'S PAPER STILL HERE.* "Mae says the café's got a new favorite topic. Word is she's that influencer who had the online mess. Folks like a story. They'll chew it even if it's stale."

Evan's jaw flexed. "It's none of their business."

"That's true," Bennie said, not unkind. "But true doesn't stop mouths." He shifted his grip on the shovel. "Started yesterday morning. Someone recognized her name from a screenshot floating around. By lunch, it had opinions."

Evan kept digging, the shovel biting into the ridge harder than it needed to. "What kind of opinions."

Bennie shrugged. "Same ones folks always have when they think they know a person from a rectangle. Some feel sorry for her. Some feel superior. A few are just bored." He hesitated, then added, "Someone asked Ruth if she'd be staying long."

Something in Evan went still. Not alarm. Calculation. "And Ruth?"

"Said what she always does," Bennie replied. "Guests are guests. Lodge isn't a rumor mill."

Evan nodded once. He trusted that. Still, a cold line slid down his spine that had nothing to do with the air. "Anyone pushing?"

"No," Bennie said. "Just watching. Talking. Passing it around like yesterday's pie." He glanced at Evan. "Midwinter doesn't chase. It waits."

They finished clearing the drift and checked the delivery crate. Bennie clapped Evan on the shoulder. "Ruth runs a good place," he said. "Wouldn't want it bothered. I'll say something if the talk turns ugly."

Evan didn't trust himself to answer, so he just nodded and started back.

He took the long way along the lake path, shovel dragging behind him. The day had softened, sun climbing higher. Frost on the pines glittered like tiny lanterns.

The lake stretched silent and white, its frozen surface marbled with faint blue veins. He paused at the edge of the trees. Across the snow, Ember Lodge sat against the slope, wood and stone and smoke curling steady. From here it looked small. Peaceful. Alive.

When he'd first started working there, it had felt like a tomb. He'd filled the quiet with repairs because repairs didn't leave you. Repairs didn't die on an icy curve five miles south of town. Repairs didn't make promises and break them.

But lately, the lodge sounded different.

Lila's laugh. The scratch of her pencil. The creak of the kitchen stool when she sat at the window. Even Juniper's demanding meow had started to feel like proof the place was meant to be lived in.

He flexed his injured hand and winced. The scrape burned, but he didn't mind. She'd patched it carefully, steady hands, worried eyes. The memory tightened his chest. He glanced down at the bandage and realized the real sting wasn't the cut.

It was the thought of someone coming in here and turning her into a headline again.

He swallowed. "Careful," he said, softer.

But careful wasn't enough.

When he reached the lodge steps, he knocked snow from his boots and went inside. Warmth met him like an embrace. Firelight flickered against the logs. Cinnamon clung faintly from breakfast.

Walter looked up from the crossword. "Did you slay the great snow ridge of the Outpost?"

"Bennie's drive is clear," Evan said. "No injuries reported."

"Good man." Walter's gaze dropped to Evan's bandaged wrist. "Except maybe one."

"Occupational hazard."

"Ah," Walter said, voice innocent as a hymn. "The kind caused by female distraction?"

Evan's ears warmed. "Just a hammer slip."

Walter's mouth quirked. "Sure it was." Then, like he hadn't just poked a bruise, he added, "Ruth says the camera in the guest hall needs a new SD card before tomorrow, or we'll lose the week's footage."

Evan stopped. "Why would we care about the footage when there's only one guest here?"

Walter stared at him over his paper. "Insurance. We've had to use footage before." He nodded toward the hall. "And because Ruth likes routine."

Evan nodded once, already deciding something else. "I'll handle it."

He poured coffee, but his attention drifted to the kitchen window. Outside, Lila crossed the courtyard bundled tight, hair tucked into her hat. She carried a small bucket and broom, leaving neat prints behind her.

She swept the porch steps, stopping every few strokes to look up at the mountains like she was trying to memorize them. The wind skittered dry needles across the boards and tugged at the loose corner of the south gutter. Another note for later. Melt always found the seam.

When she looked up and caught him watching through the glass, she smiled.

Not wide. Not performative. Just a small curve that hit somewhere deep.

He lifted his hand in greeting. She mimed wiping sweat from her brow in exaggerated exhaustion. He laughed, and it came easier than it should have.

He didn't wait for his brain to talk him out of it. He went to the mudroom and stepped outside.

"Hey," she said, cheeks pink from the cold. "Driveway's clear?"

"Clear enough for Bennie to start new gossip before lunch."

"I'm sure he already has," she said, brushing snow from her sleeve. "How's the hand?"

He flexed his fingers. "Still attached."

"Good. I didn't want my first medical intervention to end in amputation."

He smiled, but the warmth didn't reach his eyes this time. Not fully.

She noticed. She always noticed more than she said. "What happened?"

He hesitated. This was the moment. The choice. He could keep it to himself, let the quiet hold a little longer. Or he could tell her the truth and risk tightening the walls she was only just beginning to lean against.

He chose truth.

"People in town are starting to talk," he said.

The broom handle went still in her hands. The smile faded into something careful, practiced. "About what?"

"About you," he said. "Not in a cruel way. Not yet. Just... noticing. Passing it around."

She exhaled slowly. "How?"

"The way small towns do," Evan said. "A name recognized. A story half-remembered. Opinions before facts." He paused. "Bennie said it picked up yesterday. Someone asked Ruth how long you were staying."

Lila's face sagged. She forced her shoulders to loosen like she could shake it off. "It's fine. Small towns talk."

"It's not fine," Evan said, sharper than he meant. He breathed in, exhaled. Softer. "I'm sorry. I don't want anyone turning you into something you didn't agree to be."

Her eyes lifted to his, and for a second she looked startled. Not by the words. By the fact that he'd said them out loud.

"You don't owe me protection," she said, voice careful.

"I know," he said. "But I'm offering it anyway."

Snow slid off the roof somewhere above with a soft whoosh, like the lodge exhaling.

Lila nodded once, slow. "Okay," she said. "Then I'll offer you something back."

"What?"

She swallowed. "The truth. Not all of it," she admitted. "Not yet. But enough."

Evan held still. "I can handle enough."

Her breath fogged between them. "When it blew up online... I didn't just disappear because I was tired. I disappeared because I was scared." Her grip tightened on the broom. "Not of people hating me. I can handle strangers. I was scared of what it did to me. How fast I started changing to survive it. I don't want to turn into someone I don't recognize just to stay relevant."

Evan's chest tightened. He didn't reach for her. He didn't crowd her. But he stayed close enough to be real.

"I don't want to do that again," she said. "I don't want to become a version of myself I can't recognize."

"You won't," he said, and this time it wasn't a promise he made lightly. It was a decision.

She looked down, then back up, a small, shaky smile trying to return. "Thank you for fixing the roof."

"Just doing my job."

"Yeah," she said quietly. "But you didn't have to let me help."

He looked at her then, really looked. "You didn't let me do it alone," he said. "That's harder than it sounds."

Color rose in her cheeks, and she nudged a drift with her boot like she needed somewhere to put the feeling.

"Roof's holding," he said. "No more leaks for now."

"Good," she said. "Maybe we earned a break."

They stood there, cold bright around them, and for a long moment neither spoke. The world narrowed to the hush of snow and the steady rhythm of their breath.

He wanted to say it. The thing he'd been holding behind careful.

I want you here. I want this.

Words felt too big. So he chose a smaller truth that still moved them forward.

"Come by the lake later," he said, softer. "Sun sets over the ridge. Ice catches the light. Looks like the world's holding its breath."

Her gaze searched his face. "You go there a lot?"

"Sometimes," he said. "When I need to remember quiet doesn't mean lonely."

Her smile turned slow, deliberate. "I'll come by."

He nodded once. A promise tucked inside the gesture. Then he stepped back, giving her space to finish sweeping.

But he didn't go inside right away.

He stayed on the porch a few seconds longer, watching her make neat strokes with the broom like she could sweep the last of yesterday out of her body. He watched her pause, look up at the mountains, and inhale like she was learning how to breathe again.

And for the first time in years, the quiet didn't feel like armor.

It felt like anticipation.

Chapter 21

The world had changed overnight.

When Lila stepped onto the porch that morning, sunlight flooded the valley, dazzling off the snow like someone had scattered diamonds across Midwinter. The blizzard had broken before dawn, leaving behind a stillness so deep it made her chest ache. For days, gray skies had pressed down like a lid. Now the sky opened wide and blue, and the air smelled impossibly clean, pine and cold, with the faintest trace of woodsmoke rising from the chimney like proof that warmth could still be made by hand.

She tipped her face toward the sun and let her eyes close.

The light wasn't warm, not really. It didn't melt the cold so much as brighten it. But after so many dim winter days, it felt like hope with temperature. The kind that didn't ask for anything. The kind that didn't come with a caption.

Behind her, the lodge creaked as it adjusted to the sudden shift in cold. Timber settling. A soft tick from a pipe. The quiet sound of a building coming back to itself. Ruth's laughter drifted from the kitchen, Walter's voice joining in with a punchline she couldn't quite catch. Someone had put on the radio, the signal fuzzy, static mixed with old country tunes. Juniper prowled the hallway like she'd been restored to her rightful throne, tail high, opinion sharp. The whole building seemed to exhale after holding its breath through the storm.

Lila leaned on the railing and watched the valley. The snow was so bright it almost hurt, the lake beyond the trees a smooth sheet of white with faint blue shadows where the ice dipped and shifted. The world looked scrubbed clean, like it had been rinsed and hung out to dry.

Her phone sat inside on the entry table, dead as it had been for days. The thought of it didn't spike her pulse anymore. That alone felt like a miracle.

Footsteps crunched from the side path.

Evan appeared with a battered wooden sled tucked under his arm and a scarf looped haphazardly around his neck like he'd grabbed it without thinking. Sunlight turned his hair a softer brown, and the lines around his eyes eased in the brightness. He looked like himself and someone younger at the same time, as if the storm had shaken dust off the version of him that existed before careful became his default setting.

"Morning," he said, squinting against the glare. His breath fogged in front of him and vanished. "Ruth says we're officially snowbound with power lines still down in the next valley. So, in the interest of morale..." He held up the sled.

Lila stared at it, then at him. "You're joking."

"Nope." His mouth tipped at one corner. "Walter says there's a hill behind the maintenance shed that used to be the terror of Midwinter back in the sixties. I figured we should test it before he challenges us to a race."

"I thought you were the responsible one here," she said, even as laughter rose in her throat.

"Responsible, yes." His eyes warmed. "Fun-deficient, no."

He offered her a second sled, smaller and older, the paint worn to bare wood. It wasn't pretty. It was real. The kind of thing a kid would fight for anyway. She ran a gloved hand along its surface, and a ripple of nostalgia stirred like something waking up.

"This looks like the kind I used to beg my dad to take out after the first snow," she said.

"Then you'll know how to steer," he said, and there was something gentle in it, like he liked the idea of her having a past that wasn't online.

She rolled her eyes. "I knew how to steer when I weighed sixty pounds and fear was optional."

"Fear's never optional," he said. "You just learn what you're willing to do with it."

That landed deeper than he probably meant, and she swallowed, suddenly aware of how the porch felt different when he was standing beside her. Not crowded. Not tense. Just present.

He jerked his chin toward the back field. "Come on."

They trudged through knee-deep snow, laughing as they sank with every other step. Evan used his shovel to pack a trail, his boots squeaking with each lift. Lila followed, cheeks stinging, breath fogging the air. The cold found every gap in her layers and still it didn't bother her. It felt honest. Like she could trust it. Cold was cold. It didn't pretend to be something else to get a reaction.

By the time they reached the slope, she was winded and exhilarated, the kind of tired that felt earned instead of drained.

The hill wasn't steep, but the powder gleamed beneath the bright sky. Trees framed the run in dark green, and beyond them the frozen lake shimmered like a mirror waiting for someone brave enough to step onto it. Evan anchored the sleds at the top and looked back at her with a grin that made him look unguarded.

"Ready?" he asked.

"For humiliation? Always."

He laughed, set his sled first, and pushed off.

Snow sprayed as he careened down the slope, boots lifted, balance perfect. He leaned into the turn, sliding to a stop at the bottom in a smooth arc like he'd done it a hundred times. He looked up, triumphant, scarf flapping against his chest. "Your turn!"

Lila climbed onto her sled, gripping the rope handle. "This is a terrible idea!" she shouted, then shoved off before she could change her mind.

The sled shot forward.

Cold air bit her cheeks, wind tugged her hat half off, and the ground blurred beneath her. She couldn't stop laughing, not polite laughter, not careful laughter, but the real kind that burst from somewhere deep and surprised her on the way out. The sled veered, snow spraying her face, and she squealed like she was eight again and no one could embarrass her.

At the bottom, she rolled off into the drift beside Evan, gasping and grinning like she hadn't in years. Her breath came hard and fast, and her face hurt from smiling.

Evan crouched beside her and brushed snow off her shoulder with a careful hand. Not possessive. Not lingering. Attentive.

"Not bad," he said. "Points for enthusiasm."

"I'll take it." She tugged her hat straight, loose curls clinging to her collar. She started to say something joking, but what came out was quieter. "I forgot how good it feels to..."

"To be ridiculous?" he offered.

"To stop worrying," she said softly.

His smile faded into something more honest. "You're allowed. World's still spinning even when we're not documenting it."

She glanced at him. "You read my blog?"

His eyes shifted, not guilty, thoughtful. "I read the one about the lighthouse on the Oregon coast," he said. "You wrote that the silence there felt heavy. That you didn't know how to be still without feeling lost."

Her breath caught, sharp in her chest. "That was a long time ago."

"Still true?" he asked.

Lila sat up, brushing snow from her knees. "No," she said. "Not anymore." And she realized she meant it.

Something eased in his posture, like a knot loosening. He didn't say told you so. He didn't take credit. He nodded, like her truth mattered.

They made three more runs, laughing harder each time. Evan started trying to throw her off by "accidentally" bumping her sled at the top.

"You are absolutely doing that on purpose," she called over her shoulder.

"Wind," he said, deadpan, and pushed off before she could argue.

She retaliated by stealing his scarf on the next run and wearing it like a victory banner until he caught her at the bottom, breathless and grinning, and tugged it back, fingers brushing her glove.

The contact sent a sharp spark through her chest. Her heart skipped—not metaphorically, but a real, disorienting hitch—followed by a rush of heat that had nothing to do with exertion or the cold. She laughed to cover it, breath coming too fast, pulse suddenly loud in her ears.

Each time their hands met after that, the jolt came quicker, deeper, like her body was paying attention before she could tell it not to, like the cold air couldn't quite get between them anymore.

On the last run, she hit a drift at the wrong angle and toppled sideways, landing in a ridiculous heap of snow and limbs. Evan was there immediately, one hand firm on her elbow, the other bracing her back.

For a second, she forgot the cold entirely.

"Are you hurt?" he asked, voice serious now.

"No," she said breathlessly. "Mildly humbled."

His eyes held hers for a second longer than necessary. "Good," he said, and it sounded like he meant more than her elbow.

Then Ruth's voice called from the porch, loud enough to cut across the yard. "Lunch in twenty, before you both freeze solid!"

Evan lifted his head and shouted back, "Yes, ma'am!"

Lila laughed. "You called her ma'am."

"She's terrifying," he said.

"She's five-foot-two and bakes biscuits."

"That's why," he said, and she laughed again, the sound bright against the snow.

They trudged back toward the lodge with their sleds dragging behind them like childhood itself. Lila's legs ached. Her lungs felt clean. Her cheeks burned with cold and happiness. She couldn't remember the last time she'd felt tired in a way that didn't come with dread.

Inside, warmth hit in waves. The great room smelled of chicken noodle soup and bread, and the fire in the hearth roared high. She peeled off her gloves, flexing tingling fingers, watching blood return to her knuckles like color coming back to a photograph.

Evan hung their coats by the door, his hair damp from melted snow. The bandage on his wrist was clean and neat. She felt a small, stupid swell of satisfaction about that, like she'd done something right.

Juniper trotted over, tail up, as if checking that her humans hadn't abandoned her. Lila scooped the cat into her arms, laughing when Juniper protested and wriggled free with offended dignity.

Ruth appeared from the kitchen, wiping her hands on a towel. "Well, look at you two. Faces red as apples. I'd say you found a better use for the morning than moping about the power."

Evan chuckled. "Consider it field testing for the lodge's recreational amenities."

"Just don't break a leg," Ruth said. "Insurance paperwork's murder."

Walter lifted his spoon. "If you break something, at least do it dramatically. I enjoy a good story."

Evan rolled his eyes, but his smile stayed.

When they finally sat down with bowls of soup, Lila felt something settle inside her.

Not exhaustion. Not even simple contentment.

Something quieter.

The kind of peace that comes when you stop fighting your own solitude and start realizing it can be shared without being stolen. She caught herself watching Evan across the table, the way he listened more than he spoke, the way he made space around his silence instead of using it as a wall. He looked up at the exact moment she did and held her gaze, not flinching, not filling it with a joke.

It made her stomach tip, soft and unfamiliar.

By late afternoon, the light shifted again. The sun dipped behind the ridge, casting the world in soft gold. They stood at the window together as the first stars appeared, pinpricks of cold fire against the blue.

Then the lights flickered, once, twice, and stayed on.

Ruth gasped in the kitchen. Walter cheered like his team had won the Super Bowl. Somewhere down the hall, a heater clicked to life, humming like a sigh of relief.

Lila blinked at the sudden brightness, the hum of electricity filling the hush that had become familiar. The lodge sounded different instantly. Less like a secret. More like the world returning with its expectations.

She glanced at Evan.

He was watching the ceiling lights with an expression caught between surprise and something else. Not anger. Not even disappointment, exactly.

Regret.

Like part of him had liked the dark because it gave them an excuse to stay close to the fire and call it practical.

"Feels strange, doesn't it?" she said.

He nodded slowly. "We got used to the dark."

"Or maybe we remembered how to see in it," she said quietly.

His gaze shifted to her then, and it wasn't cautious. It was steady. Like he was choosing to stand here instead of retreating to the safe work of fixing and checking and avoiding.

"Power being back doesn't change what happened," she said before she could talk herself out of it. The words came out softer than she intended, but they didn't break. "It doesn't erase it."

His throat moved. He looked away for half a second, then back. "No," he said. "It doesn't."

The lights reflected in the window, twin halos hovering over their silhouettes. For the first time since she'd arrived in Midwinter, she didn't feel like a guest.

She felt like part of something. A story still being written, one soft moment at a time.

Evan looked over, met her eyes, and smiled.

Not the cautious smile from before. A real one, open and sure, full of quiet promise.

The storm had passed, the power was back, and the world had changed again.

This time, she was ready for it.

Chapter 22

The hum of electricity filled the lodge again, soft but startling.

For days, the silence had been complete, broken only by the crackle of fire, the shuffle of boots, the sigh of snow against the windows. Now the heaters buzzed, the lights glowed, and somewhere in the kitchen the old refrigerator groaned awake like a creature dragged out of hibernation. The lodge didn't just sound different, it felt different.

Evan stood by the window, a mug of coffee cooling in his hand, and watched Lila's reflection shimmer beside his own. She was turned toward the glass, eyes bright with wonder and something he recognized too well.

Reluctance.

Wanting something always did that to people. Lit them up. Made them visible.

"It's strange," she said, voice low, like she didn't want to spook the moment. "All this noise."

He nodded once. "You'd think we'd missed it."

"Maybe we did." Her mouth curved faintly. "But now it feels louder than it used to."

"That's because we stopped mistaking quiet for emptiness," he said, and the words surprised him with how true they sounded.

She turned toward him, and the room went still in a different way. The lights hummed overhead, the kind of small mechanical sound that once meant routine. Now it sounded like change.

From the entry table, a sound cut through the room. A thin electronic chirp, too cheerful for a place that had been living by firelight. Lila froze. Her gaze flicked toward it.

Her phone.

It sat there like an animal that had woken up hungry.

Another chirp. Then a second. Then a rapid stutter as notifications stacked, the screen glowing brighter with each one.

Evan watched her shoulders tighten. The shift was subtle, but he'd learned to notice subtle. Subtle was the first warning before weather turned.

She didn't move. She didn't reach for it. For a moment, he thought she might pretend it wasn't happening. That she might keep standing here with him, held in the small safe world they'd built in the dark.

Then she exhaled and said, too casually, "Well. There it is."

"The world?" he asked.

"My old life," she corrected, and he heard the effort it took to keep her voice steady.

The phone buzzed again, a longer vibration this time, like insistence. She flinched, then looked up at him with something close to apology in her eyes.

"I should..." Her gaze slid back to the table. "I should check it."

He could have told her she didn't have to. He could have been the man who said, Stay. Let it wait. We'll keep the quiet a little longer.

Instead, he did what he always did when something mattered.

He made space.

"Yeah," he said, voice even. "You should."

It was the right answer and it tasted wrong in his mouth.

Lila's eyes lingered on him, searching his face for judgment, for disappointment, for anything that would tell her what this meant. He held his expression still, careful not to show how much it meant that she'd hesitated at all.

She crossed the room slowly, like each step was a decision. She picked up the phone with two fingers, as if it might bite her, and the screen lit her face in harsh white.

Evan didn't see the words, but he saw the effect. The way her throat worked. The way her smile tried to appear and failed.

"It's a lot," she said quietly.

He set his mug down before his grip cracked the ceramic. "Anything urgent?"

She swallowed. Her thumb hovered over the screen, not scrolling, not opening, holding back the flood. "No. Just reminders. People. Messages I didn't ask for." A humorless laugh. "And a couple I did."

He felt the instinct to step closer, to take the phone out of her hand and toss it into the snow. Not because he thought he could save her, but because he understood the way noise could claw until thoughts faded.

He didn't move.

Distance felt safer.

Ruth called from the kitchen, loud and bright. "Anybody want pie before the power goes out again? I'm not waiting on the grid to decide if it likes us today."

Lila blinked, like the voice pulled her back into her body. "Pie," she said, and the word sounded like a lifeline.

She turned the phone face down and left it on the table, a small act of rebellion that made something in Evan's chest loosen.

When she came back with a plate, she handed him a fork. "Ruth says this is the celebration course."

"What are we celebrating?" he asked, though he already knew the answer wasn't just electricity.

"The lights. The heat. Survival." She shrugged. "Take your pick."

He accepted the fork, and the brush of her skin against his knuckles sent a faint pulse through him. He kept his hand still, afraid any movement might ask for more than he could afford.

They sat side by side near the fire. Juniper occupied the armrest, tail curled like punctuation, eyes half-lidded in judgment.

Evan took a bite of pie. The crust was still warm, buttery and sweet, and the taste hit him like a memory he hadn't realized he still carried. "Apple cinnamon," he said. "My grandmother used to make this."

Lila smiled, softer now. "Guess Ruth knows her audience."

"She always does," he said, and something about the way Lila looked at him made him feel exposed. Not in a bad way. In a way he didn't know how to protect himself from.

The lights flickered once, dimming the room to amber before brightening again. Firelight mingled with lamplight, painting the walls in soft gold. For the first time, the lodge didn't feel like a place he worked.

It felt like a place he belonged.

Belonging was dangerous. You only lost things you let yourself have.

Lila leaned back, legs curled beneath her. Her eyes drifted to the window, where snow caught the reflection of the lamps in faint halos. "It feels different now," she said quietly. "Like the storm changed something, and the light just showed us what's left."

"Storms usually do," Evan said. "They strip things down. You see what matters when you've got nothing else to distract you."

"And what matters to you?" she asked.

He felt the old reflex rise, fast and familiar. Say something safe. Something practical. The roof. The generator. Keeping the guests warm. Say the replaceable things.

But the truth waited in his chest, patient and persistent, and he was tired of being a man who only spoke in repairs.

"Peace," he said finally. "I didn't realize I'd been chasing it until this week." He stared at his bandaged wrist, at the neat work she'd done there. "Thought I wanted quiet. Turns out I wanted stillness that didn't feel lonely."

He didn't say her name. He didn't have to.

Lila's eyes softened, and it hit him how easily she could turn that softness into a knife without meaning to. All she'd have to do is leave.

"That's exactly what I've been looking for, too," she whispered.

The air between them shifted, warmer, more certain. The distance that had held them apart thinned into something fragile, almost transparent.

Fragile things broke first.

"Funny," he said, voice low, trying for humor and landing on honesty. "I thought I came here to fix things."

"Maybe you did," she said, smiling gently. "Just not the ones you expected."

He let out a quiet laugh that caught in his throat. He knew then he would pull back. Not because he didn't want her, but because he did. Wanting was the part that made you stupid.

"You make it sound simple," he said.

"It isn't." She glanced toward the entry table where her phone sat like a closed eye. "But it's worth trying."

He looked at her hand on her plate, the faint tremor that came and went like a heartbeat. Without thinking, he reached out and covered her fingers with his, just briefly, just enough to steady.

Her breath hitched.

He felt it. Felt the way the moment leaned forward, hungry.

He should have let his hand fall away.

Instead, he held on for one more beat, and his voice came out rougher than he meant. "If you leave," he said, then stopped. Because saying it would make it real.

Lila didn't pull her hand away. She turned her palm up slightly, inviting instead of demanding. "If I leave," she said softly, "it won't be because you weren't enough."

That was the problem. He didn't trust enough. He didn't trust that good things didn't come with an ending hidden inside them.

Outside, the last of the sunlight bled away, leaving only the soft shimmer of reflected snow. Inside, the lights hummed steady, the fire settled low, and for a long while neither of them spoke.

He stayed still, careful not to reach for what might disappear if he named it.

When Ruth called them for tea, Lila stood, brushing imaginary crumbs from her jeans. She paused by the table and glanced at her phone again, face unreadable.

Then she looked back at Evan. "Tomorrow we should walk to the lake," she said. "You can show me that spot where the ice catches the light."

He rose slowly, the corners of his mouth lifting, a smile he didn't have to force. "You remembered."

"I remember everything that sounds like a promise," she said.

That was exactly why he didn't make one. He didn't trust his voice enough to answer. He only nodded, the safest agreement he knew how to give.

Lila smiled as if his nod was enough. Then she disappeared toward the kitchen, carrying her plate like it wasn't suddenly too heavy.

Evan lingered by the window, snow outside silvered under the moonlight. The power lines stretched like thin veins against the dark, carrying warmth back into the valley.

Maybe the power coming back wasn't the end of the storm.

Maybe it was the moment right before you learned what wanting could cost.

And the worst part was, he wasn't sure he wanted to stop wanting.

Chapter 23

T he morning began with silence that carried weight
instead of peace.

Snowlight pressed through the curtains in a pale wash,
soft as milk but cold around the edges. Lila sat cross-legged
on the bed, laptop open, her stomach tightening with
every line of the email on the screen. The glow made her
skin look washed out, as if even the machine sensed what
she didn't want to face.

From: Dana Carlisle

Subject: URGENT: Unauthorized Posts

Lila,

We finally figured out what happened.

*Your assistant had been editing your posts using AI tools
without telling you. She believed your recent drafts weren't
"landing" and thought she was protecting your brand by
cleaning them up.*

I know. I'm furious, too.

We've pulled the logs and can prove the uploads didn't come from you. The problem is... the story already ran. Retractions don't travel as far as accusations.

I know you want to step back until it cools off, but I think we need to fight this.

– D

She read it twice, then a third time. AI-generated filler. The phrase tasted like poison. She had walked away from that world to escape the churn, the ghost-written blur that had drained the joy from words. Now her name sat on something hollow and smiling, pretending to be her.

Another ping.

I've issued a partial retraction, but we need a quote from you. If you don't respond, it looks like guilt by silence.

Guilt by silence.

She closed the laptop and pressed her palms to her eyes until her vision speckled. She wasn't guilty, not exactly, but she wasn't innocent either. She had let the assistant handle updates. She had told herself it was responsible, that delegation was healthy, that she deserved to sleep through a morning without composing a caption in her head. She had trusted the system to keep her brand alive while she tried to recover her humanity. The machine had filled space with something that sounded almost right until it wasn't.

And people didn't care about almost.

Her throat tightened as the old reflex rose, hard and fast. Fix it. Explain. Perform remorse. Be likeable while you bleed.

She stared at the laptop's closed lid like it might open on its own and start writing the apology for her.

Juniper hopped onto the blanket and circled twice before settling against Lila's thigh, purring as if the world hadn't shifted. The cat's steady warmth grounded her for a breath. Then the laptop chimed again, insistent, and her pulse climbed like it had found a familiar staircase.

She opened the laptop with a wince, as if the hinge hurt.

On instinct, she checked the top right corner. Signal. Two bars. Enough to be dangerous.

She typed anyway.

Dana—

I'm in a remote location with limited service. I didn't authorize her to use AI to edit those posts. She was only supposed to check spelling and grammar before posting. I'll take responsibility for oversight but not authorship. Please remove them entirely. I'll issue my own statement once I've had time to—

Once I've had time to what?

Think. Hide. Decide if she could survive watching strangers dissect her integrity like it was a product review.

She sat there with the cursor blinking at her like a dare. The words she'd started suddenly felt wrong, too careful, too corporate. Oversight. Authorship. Statement. Language that made a human problem sound like a manageable task.

She saved the draft and shut the computer. The click felt final, like a door in a house you weren't sure you wanted to leave.

Outside, a shovel scraped the deck in a steady rhythm. Evan, clearing the steps. The sound usually soothed her. Today it carved through the quiet like accusation. Because he was doing something real. Because he was solving a problem with his hands and not his image.

She glanced at the clock. 11:22.

Too early to have answers. Too late to pretend this wasn't happening.

Her phone buzzed again, then again. She didn't pick it up. She didn't want to see which part of her life had woken up first, the professional one or the panicked one.

The drip from the night before had stopped, but she could still see the faint ring on the plaster near the corner, a bruise of water that would dry and leave a stain. Proof that even small disasters marked you.

A knock. Two short taps, one longer. Evan's rhythm.

"Come in."

He stood in the doorway, cheeks red from the cold, scarf tucked under his jacket, hair damp at the ends. He looked as he always did, steady and real, but his eyes softened when they landed on her.

"Hey," he said. "You okay?"

"Yeah." The word came out thin. "Emails."

"The kind that make you look like you've been staring at a wall for an hour?"

"Something like that." Her laugh tried and failed. She started to tell him, to let him know what was happening, but she couldn't find the words. She was angry, embarrassed, and confused. How could she explain it? She'd hired her assistant, but it was her responsibility to make sure the job was being done correctly. Wasn't it? Yes, she should have been able to trust the young woman to do as was expected of her, but at the end of the day, it was Lila's name on the line. She should have verified the content before it went live.

He stepped in farther, not crowding her, but closing the distance enough that she could smell winter on him. Pine and cold air. A hint of coffee. His gaze flicked once to the shut laptop.

He didn't ask what it said.

Evan had a way of not forcing. It wasn't indifference. It was respect. And respect made lying feel impossible, so she didn't lie. She redirected.

"Did the plow come through?" she asked.

"Early. Road's open again. Power's holding." His mouth tipped into a faint smile. "The world's back online."

The phrase landed heavy.

"Back online," she echoed, aiming for light and missing it.

"You look tired," he said.

"I didn't sleep much."

"Too much coffee?"

"Too many thoughts."

Concern shadowed the edges of his smile. "You've been quiet since last night."

"Just thinking about what comes next."

"After the snow clears?" he asked, and the way he said it made her feel like he was talking about more than roads.

"Something like that."

He nodded slowly, like he was building a bridge she wasn't crossing. "If you need to head back soon, I get it. You've probably got people waiting."

Something twisted inside her, sharp and unfair. She should have corrected him. She should have told him the truth. That people weren't waiting like he meant. That they were circling.

She didn't.

"I'll let you get back to work," she said instead.

His eyes stayed on her for a heartbeat longer, searching her face for the thing she wasn't saying. Then he nodded once, controlled. "Right. Shout if you need me."

The door closed with a soft click, like a book snapping shut on an unfinished sentence.

Lila stared at the ceiling. The room felt too neat, too temporary, like it was trying not to be noticed. The fire downstairs had burned low, a dull orange glow that barely reached the corners. Juniper slipped to the sill and watched the snow as if she expected the day to behave.

Lila opened the laptop again, half-expecting more urgency.

The same subject lines waited.

RE: Statement Required.

Follow-up.

Sponsor escalation.

Her throat tightened. She typed a new line in the draft.

I need a few days before I respond publicly.

She backspaced.

She couldn't promise days. She didn't know what she would say. She didn't know who she could be without smoothing the edges for public consumption.

Her phone buzzed. The signal had steadied.

A text from Dana: *This might go viral. Please get ahead of it.*

The words blurred. She set the phone down and pressed the heels of her hands to her forehead until the ache distracted her from the panic. Outside, the shovel scraped again. The sound should have comforted her. It only widened the space between them.

By late morning, she wandered downstairs, hungry for distraction and warmth. The great room smelled of yeast and cinnamon. Ruth stood at the counter, humming while she kneaded bread dough, her hands moving with calm authority. Flour dusted her cardigan like a careless snowfall.

"Morning, dear," Ruth said. "You and Evan planning another sled run?"

"I think I'm retiring undefeated," Lila said automatically.

"Well, that's the best time to quit." Ruth dusted her hands and studied Lila's face in a way that felt like being seen without being cornered. "You look troubled. Want to talk about it?"

"Just work things," Lila said. "It's nothing."

Ruth made a sound that was half amusement, half warning. "Nothing is usually something with a different name." She slid the pan into the oven and leaned her hip against the counter. "Whatever it is, don't let it steal what you've found here. The world will wait. It always does."

Lila wanted to believe that. The world she had left behind never waited. It replaced. It filled any gap with noise and then blamed you for not being loud enough.

She thanked Ruth and slipped outside before her eyes could betray her.

The air had sharpened, sun filtered through thin cloud. Melt had started in small places, a slow drip from the eaves, a faint glitter on the roofline. She followed the sound of hammering to the woodshed.

Evan was repairing a cracked panel, movements steady and precise, shoulders squared against the cold. Each strike had purpose. When he saw her, the rhythm faltered for half a second before continuing, as if he'd trained himself not to show how much her presence changed his day.

"Hey," she said.

"Hey." He didn't stop working.

"I didn't mean to interrupt."

"You're not." He drove another nail. "Trying to finish before the next freeze."

She folded her arms, wishing she knew what to say. She wanted to tell him about the emails, the accusations, the old fear that her life was built on an illusion. Every sentence she rehearsed sounded like an excuse. Like she wanted him to reassure her. Like she was asking him to carry something he hadn't agreed to hold.

So she said nothing.

"You were right," he said after a moment, voice quiet enough that she almost missed it. "About storms changing things."

"What do you mean?"

He set the hammer down and wiped his gloves against his jeans. His breath fogged and vanished. "When power came back last night, it felt like we lost something." He stared past her, toward the lodge. "Like the quiet belonged to another world."

Her chest tightened. "Evan—"

He lifted a hand, not to stop her, just to steady himself. "I guess I thought..." He let it go, swallowing the rest. "Doesn't matter."

"It does," she said, and she meant it. She meant him. She meant the week of warmth that had started to feel like a place she could stand.

He shook his head once, small. "You've got your life out there. I can see it in your face when you check your phone." His voice stayed careful, but the honesty cut. "I don't blame you. But I don't want to mistake this," he gestured between them, small and real, "for something it's not."

The words hit harder than she expected, because part of her had been hoping he would do exactly that. Mistake it. Claim it. Make it easy.

She opened her mouth to deny it, to tell him he was wrong, to insist she wasn't leaving. But guilt crowded her throat, thick and heavy.

Because she didn't know.

Because she hadn't told him the truth.

Because he was reading her silence the only way he could.

He studied her a beat longer, waiting for an answer she couldn't give. Quiet acceptance settled into his features, and the change in him was immediate, like a latch clicking shut.

"Take care of what you need to," he said. "I'll be around."

He picked up the hammer again. The finality in the movement said more than the words.

Lila stood there a moment longer, listening to each strike echo in her chest, and realized she had done the thing she hated most.

She had made someone feel like an option.

She turned toward the lodge. The path looked longer now. The cold felt sharper. She hadn't meant to hurt him, but intention didn't change impact.

Silence, she realized, could wound deeper than truth.

Inside, the bread had begun to rise, swelling softly beneath a towel like something hopeful. Warmth floated from the oven. She sat at the kitchen table and opened her laptop.

The screen's cold light swallowed the room's warmth whole.

Subject lines waited like accusations.

RE: Statement Required.

Please confirm by noon.

Her hands hovered over the keyboard, shaking just enough that she clenched them into fists.

For once, she had no words.

And the worst part was, she finally understood what Evan meant.

Storms didn't only knock out power.

Sometimes they knocked loose the parts of you that had been holding by habit.

She stared at the blinking cursor until it felt like a heartbeat.

Then, slowly, she typed a new first line.

I owe you the truth.

She didn't hit send.

Not yet.

But the sentence sat there on the screen, steady and unpretty, and for the first time all morning, it felt like the beginning of doing it right.

Chapter 24

Evan worked until the rhythm drowned everything else out.

Nail. Set. Strike. The sound cracked the cold air and scattered into the trees. He fixed the split board along the shed wall, hands sure, movements small and tidy. Work made sense. If he held the line straight, if he kept the grain under his palm, if he did the ordinary thing correctly, then chaos had fewer ways in.

Except it had already found one.

He had seen it in the way Lila stood there with her arms folded, eyes somewhere he couldn't follow. He had offered a bridge and left it hanging between them. He'd meant it as a kindness. It had landed like distance.

Boots crunched behind him.

"Board's true," Walter said, nodding at the line of nails. "Won't even see the patch come spring."

"Won't matter if we keep the roof dry." Evan brushed sawdust from his gloves and checked the seam with his thumb. "Wind's shifting. If it swings north, we'll get a drift at the back corner."

"Might." Walter studied him with a father's patience, like he could see the weather in Evan's face, too. "Ruth says the stew's better on the second warm. Lila ate like a bird at lunch. Not like her."

"Something came up."

"Work?"

"Seems like it."

Walter's mouth tipped, sympathetic without prying. "We keep the coffee hot whether folks are talking or not."

"I know."

They stood a few breaths together, listening to winter settle. When Walter wandered off, quiet returned. Not the warm kind Evan had come to like this week. The other kind, the kind that hummed under the skin.

He swept the bench, hung the hammer, and walked the path to the lake. The snow was packed by boots and runner tracks. Juniper's prancing prints stitched the edge, small and arrogant. Farther down, the trail smoothed to a clean white ribbon, untouched, like the world had decided to start over.

The lake waited as always, a broad, frozen plain with faint blue veins under the surface. Pines darkened the far shore. He stood at the clearing and looked across the ice. Yesterday, he had pictured standing here with Lila, pointing out the place where the late sun shattered into a thousand shards. He had pictured her tipping her head like she was listening for something beneath the surface.

He had not pictured the empty space.

He sat on a fallen log and let the quiet do what it always did. Winter wore you down by degrees until what remained was honest. He thought of old fractures, slow erasing rather than slammed doors. Better to fix things alone, he had decided back then. Better not to want what asked to be tended.

He had not planned on Lila. Not the way she stayed still in the hush. Not the way she laughed on the hill, unguarded as falling. Not the quick shutter of her face when the outside world knocked.

He rubbed his wrist. The scrape had faded to a thin line. The ache was useful. Contained. He stood when the last rake of sun caught in a jag of ice and made hope feel fragile and possible all at once.

He could press. He could ask what changed and who was pulling at her. He could also do what he'd always done when things got complicated.

Step back and call it respect.

He chose the cleaner version. Give space. Keep the roof tight. Offer small anchors and let her decide whether to tie to them.

Back at the lodge, lamps cast soft circles. The fire hummed low. Ruth looked up from folded napkins and didn't bother pretending she didn't notice the tension riding Evan's shoulders.

"You'll catch your death standing there dripping like an icicle," she said, smiling.

"Lake path's clear. I'll pack it again in the morning if the temperature drops."

"You'll do no such thing before you eat." She tipped her chin toward the stove. "Soup's on the back burner. Bread's wrapped. Her Highness is under the baking rack, so step light."

He listened for other sounds. Lila's laugh. A footfall on the stairs. Only the clink of a spoon and Walter's quiet skirmish with a crossword.

He ladled Irish stew into a bowl, cut a thick slice of bread, and ate because that is what you do when a day stretches tight. Feed the body so the mind doesn't fray.

Halfway through, light steps tapped down the hall.

Lila slid into view, hair pulled back. She held her phone like a weight she couldn't set down. The signal must have stabilized, because it buzzed again in her palm and she flinched before she could hide it.

Evan set his spoon down.

"Soup's good," he said, keeping his voice ordinary on purpose.

"Ruth is incapable of making anything else." Her smile tried to show up and didn't quite make it.

They stood close enough to share the warmth of the range, far enough to keep a careful line. He could feel the exact distance between them like a measurement he'd made with his hands. Two feet. One hard breath.

"Do you need space?" he asked.

Her brows lifted, quick. "Why?"

"So I don't put another thing on a table that already looks crowded."

She looked down at the phone, then up at him again, eyes bright in a way that wasn't good. "I don't know what I need."

He nodded, slow, so she could see he believed her. "Okay."

Her phone buzzed again, sharper. She swallowed, thumb hovering as if she might throw it across the room or answer it and lose herself. He didn't tell her what to do. He didn't offer solutions she hadn't asked for. But he couldn't do nothing.

"If it's bad," he said, "you don't have to hold it alone."

The silence that followed wasn't rejection. It was fear, turning around in her chest, looking for the safest exit.

Ruth breezed in with a tray and read them like a favorite book. She set two mugs on the counter and didn't look at either of them directly, which was its own kind of mercy.

"Tea for thoughtful faces," she said. "Honey and a bit of the good lemon."

"Thank you," Lila murmured.

They drank in silence. Lila's phone buzzed once more. She didn't check it. Evan looked away. The only thing worse than a hard choice is being witnessed while you make it.

"Evan," she said after a minute, almost too low to hear. "I didn't mean to be..."

He waited. He didn't help her finish. If she wanted to name it, she would.

"Distant," she said. "It isn't about you."

He believed her. It didn't mean it didn't touch him. "You don't owe me an explanation."

Her jaw worked, like she was holding back a confession and an apology at the same time. "Maybe not," she said. "But I don't like what this is making me."

That landed. Not because it explained the situation. Because it was a truth.

"If you need help with something practical," he said, "say it. I'm good at practical."

A small line eased near her mouth. "You are."

He rinsed his bowl and stepped back so she could breathe. "I'm going to check the south eave before it freezes. Then the generator. If you want a quieter place to think, the library nook stays warm and nobody uses it after dinner. The lamp in the corner flickers unless you wiggle the cord."

"Thank you."

He took a wool blanket from the storage closet and draped it over the arm of the library chair. He seated the lamp plug and set a small plate of shortbread on the table because Ruth always swore sugar helped thinking, and because offering food was the safest kind of care he knew.

At dusk, the patch along the eave held. Meltwater found the channel he cut. The temperature dropped and the shingles sang a faint ice song. When he came back in, the lamp in the nook glowed steady.

Lila sat curled under the blanket with her laptop, shoulders tense but not collapsed. Not the bright, brittle light of panic on her face. A steadier sort. Every so often, her hand found the mug and lifted. Like she was teaching her body to keep doing small things even when the larger things wanted to swallow her.

He stood in the doorway a beat too long, then stepped away before she felt him there like another obligation.

In the workshop, Walter oiled the snowblower chain. "Storm calendar gives us two quiet days," he said. "After that, who knows."

"Two days is enough to put the west rail back in," Evan said.

"You don't have to say it," Walter said. "Sometimes the good ones look like they might run. Sometimes they come back around."

"I'm not trying to make her stay," Evan said. "I just don't want to turn something fine into something heavy."

"Which is why you might be the one she trusts," Walter said. "People who've carried weight know how to set it down."

The words settled in Evan's chest and didn't move.

Later, he made one more pass through the hall. Old habits. He checked thermostats, banked the fire, and turned the cameras to save battery now that the grid was back. A soft click above suggested a laptop closing. He stepped onto the porch. The night had hardened into bright cold. Stars crowded the sky. The lake held them like a second heaven.

He went back in, tore a lodge card from the stack at the desk, and wrote by lamplight with the blunt honesty he used when a repair mattered.

He set the card on the library table where she would see it when she reached for the lamp.

Library lamp fixed. Blanket is wool, not scratchy.

If you need an extra hour of quiet, I can walk the loop in the morning and keep folks out of here.

If you want company, meet me at the lake at nine.

If you want neither, I'll be around.

— E.

He slept light and dreamed of ice catching light and breaking it into a hundred small fires that still belonged to the same whole.

Before dawn, he pulled on his boots and packed the path anyway. Habit and hope sometimes looked the same. The sky lifted gray at the edge. He tamped the snow until the trail settled and his breath came out slow.

At eight fifty-five, he stood at the clearing and waited. Hands in his pockets, not because he was cold but because it kept him from reaching.

The lake held the last of the night. The ridge thinned toward gold.

Bootsteps approached on packed snow. He didn't turn right away. He let the rhythm prove itself. When he finally looked over his shoulder, a figure rounded the bend. Hat pulled down. Scarf tucked. Shoulders squared as if walking into a private wind.

Lila stopped beside him and looked out. She didn't speak. Neither did he.

The sun tipped over the ridge. Light ran across the lake and shattered at a jag of ice near the middle. A scatter of bright sparks lifted in the cold air, then fell back to rest.

He felt her breath change. Not a gasp. Something quieter. A release she didn't ask permission to have.

He didn't reach for her hand. He let the sight do the talking.

"Thank you for the note," she said.

"Always."

Her voice thickened. "I might not be able to explain everything yet."

"You don't have to," he said. "Just be here when you want to be here."

She looked at him, eyes wet but steady. "I didn't correct you earlier. When you said you didn't want to mistake this." Her throat worked. "I let you think I was leaving."

"I know," he said quietly. "I heard the quiet answer."

"I'm sorry."

Restraint had always felt like strength. Tonight, it felt like risk. "I'd rather have a true silence than a pretty lie."

Her eyes closed for a second, then opened again to the light on the ice. "I'm trying not to be either."

"Good," he said. "We have time."

He meant it the way he built things, in inches, not declarations. She nodded as if that size fit her, like it didn't demand she become someone louder than she could be today.

They stood until the bright strip dulled and the day settled into ordinary cold.

When they walked back up the path, they left two clean lines behind them, parallel and close. Not crossing. Not wandering. Headed toward the same warm door.

Chapter 25

The main road had finally reopened, a narrow black ribbon carved through miles of white. The snowplow had come before dawn, its heavy treads leaving behind ridges like corduroy, and the morning sun gleamed off them in bright, blinding bands. For the first time in nearly a week, the world beyond Ember Lodge felt reachable again.

Lila pressed her forehead lightly against the passenger window as Evan steered them toward town. The truck's heater hummed, filling the cab with that dry, metallic warmth that only old vehicles could make. Snowbanks loomed high on both sides of the road, clean and sharp-edged.

It should have felt like freedom, returning to civilization after days of storm and silence, but the closer they got to Midwinter, the tighter her stomach grew.

"Feels strange, doesn't it?" Evan said, eyes on the road. "Like we've been gone longer than we have."

She smiled faintly. "It's only been a few days."

"Long enough for the world to reset itself."

She watched him as he spoke. The sunlight caught the stubble on his jaw, the easy concentration in his expression. His hand rested loosely on the gearshift, calloused and steady.

The cab was warm, but her fingers were still cold. Without thinking, she slid her hands between her thighs for heat, then hated herself for the small, childish motion.

Evan glanced over, then tugged off his gloves. He didn't look at her when he did it, like he was trying to make it casual.

"Here," he said, holding them out.

Lila blinked. "Evan, you'll freeze."

"I run hot," he lied, and his mouth tilted like he knew she'd call him on it.

She took the gloves anyway. The inside held his warmth, a faint scent of leather and cedar. She curled her fingers into it and felt her chest do something stupid and soft.

"Thank you," she said, too quietly.

His gaze flicked to her hands and back to the road. "Don't mention it."

She wanted to reach for his hand, to close the small space between them, but the guilt still sitting heavy in her chest twisted against the impulse. She didn't trust herself not to take more than he meant to offer.

They passed the sign that read, Midwinter, Montana—Pop. 1,826, half-buried in snow. Beyond it, rooftops appeared, smoke curling from chimneys, wreaths still clinging to shop doors. The town looked exactly like she remembered from her first drive through, when she'd arrived desperate for quiet and anonymity.

Now the same streets felt smaller, sharper.

Evan turned down the main stretch and parked in front of the Blue Finch Café & Book Nook, its bright blue siding a cheerful contrast to the white drifts piled against it. Through the fogged windows, Lila could see the familiar warmth of golden light and the movement of people inside, Nora West behind the counter, Mason hauling a crate of firewood through the door.

"Need coffee?" Evan asked.

"Always," she said, but her voice came out quieter than intended.

He gave her a sidelong look. "You sure you're up for this?"

She nodded quickly. "Yeah. Just feels like stepping back into the noise, that's all."

He smiled gently. "Noise isn't all bad."

Before they got out, he leaned across her just enough to reach the glove compartment. The movement brought him close, close enough that his shoulder brushed her arm, close enough that she felt heat through wool and denim and the tight awareness she'd been pretending she didn't have. He smelled like winter air and coffee and smoke.

He pulled out a knit cap and held it out.

"You forgot yours," he said.

She took it, but her fingers caught his for a second. Not accidental. Not entirely.

A pause snapped between them, thin and electric.

Lila swallowed. "Thanks."

Evan's eyes dropped to her mouth, quick as a spark, then moved away like he'd never been there at all. "Come on," he said, voice rougher than before. "It's cold."

When they stepped out of the truck, the cold hit like a slap, clean and biting. The café bell jingled as they entered, releasing a rush of cinnamon, coffee, and fresh bread. The air inside shimmered with warmth and the low buzz of conversation.

"Evan Drake!" Nora called from behind the counter, wiping her hands on a towel. "About time you came to town. I was about to send a search party."

Evan chuckled. "Just waiting for the roads to forgive us."

"Well, they finally did." She grinned at Lila, eyes curious but kind. "And who's this? I don't think we've met."

"Lila Moore," Lila said, shaking her hand. "Guest at the lodge."

"Welcome to Midwinter," Nora said. "Coffee or cocoa?"

"Coffee, please. Black."

"Adventurous," Nora teased, then slid two steaming mugs across the counter.

As they found a small table near the window, Lila felt the shift in the room, how people greeted Evan by name, how warmth seemed to follow him. He wasn't just the quiet handyman who fixed things. Here, he belonged.

A woman at the corner table asked about the lodge repairs. Another man waved and joked about the "legendary Ember roof." Evan answered each with the same calm humor she'd come to know, and something inside her tugged, half admiration, half ache.

He belonged everywhere. She belonged nowhere.

She tried to focus on her coffee, on the way the steam curled against the cold window, but the noise of conversation wrapped too tightly around her. Words like lodge and storm and internet floated through the air, and she couldn't tell if she was imagining the ones that sounded like her name.

Evan nudged her boot with his, a soft grounding tap. It wasn't flirtation. It was reassurance. It made her eyes sting anyway.

"You okay?" he asked quietly.

She nodded, grateful and ashamed at once. "Yeah."

Evan rose to pay, and she followed him toward the counter. That's when she felt it.

The entire atmosphere shifted.

The woman behind the register went still, her eyes narrowing slightly as she looked at Lila's face again. Not curiosity. Recognition catching late.

"I'm sorry," the woman said, hesitating. "Has anyone ever told you that you look just like—"

Lila's stomach dropped.

"...Lila Moore?"

The name landed softly. That almost made it worse.

Evan's hand paused on his wallet. He glanced back at Lila, a question already forming.

"I get that a lot," Lila said automatically. Too fast.

The woman tilted her head. "Travel blogger, right? You used to write about coastal towns and small places like

this." Her smile wavered, uncertain now. "My sister followed you. Still does, I think."

Heat rushed up Lila's neck.

"Oh." The woman shifted, lowering her voice, leaning
in as if they were co-conspirators instead of strangers. "Can
I ask you something? You don't have to answer."

Lila already knew she would.

"Is it true?" the woman asked. "About the AI thing?"

The word hit harder than she expected. Sharp. Clinical.
A shortcut to judgment.

"That you didn't really write your posts anymore," the
woman continued. "That someone else—or something
else—was doing it for you."

The café felt suddenly too bright. Lila became aware
of every nearby sound. Cups clinking. A chair scraping.
Someone laughing too loud.

She swallowed. "That's not what happened."

The woman nodded, quick and apologetic. "I figured.
People like simple stories." She slid the receipt across the
counter. "For what it's worth, I always liked your earlier
stuff. It felt... real."

That might have hurt more than the accusation.

Evan stepped closer without touching her. Close
enough that she could feel the warmth of him, solid and
unmistakably present.

"Ready?" he asked, his voice calm, ordinary, offering an
exit without pressure.

"Yeah," she said, though it came out thin.

As they turned away from the counter, she caught her
reflection in the glass pastry case. For a split second, she saw

herself the way the world sometimes did now—familiar, examined, slightly off. A face attached to a version of her life that no longer fit.

"I'm sorry," she said quietly as they moved toward the door. "That happens sometimes. People always think they're entitled to answers."

He met her eyes. "They're not."

She nodded, swallowing hard.

Behind them, the woman cleared her throat, embarrassed now, and busied herself rearranging cups that didn't need rearranging.

Lila's hands were shaking. Small. Traitorous.

"I didn't do it," she said, too fast. "I didn't write those posts. I wasn't even posting anymore. Someone else. My assistant."

"You don't owe me an explanation," Evan said gently.

She looked at him then. Really looked. His jaw was tight, his eyes steady. Not angry. Protective in a way that didn't demand anything back.

"They think I ran because I'm guilty," she said.

"They think whatever's easiest," he replied.

That did it. The tightness in her chest cracked just enough to hurt.

Evan shifted, angling his body so she didn't have to face the room. "Let's go," he said. Not retreat. Not escape. A choice.

She nodded.

As they stepped back into the cold, his hand hovered near her elbow—not touching, but there if she needed it.

For the first time since the rumors started, she didn't feel like she was being watched.

She felt like someone was standing between her and the noise.

"You didn't let me see any of this," he said after a moment. His voice wasn't sharp, but it carried a weight he hadn't expected to be holding.

"I was trying to start over," she said. "To get quiet. To figure out who I am without all of that."

His gaze dropped to her hands. The coffee cup trembled slightly. He reached out and wrapped his palm around the side of it, steadying it and, by extension, her. His thumb pressed once against her knuckles, a small, unconscious gesture.

The contact made her want to lean into him. It also made the space between them feel suddenly fragile. She pulled out her phone and texted Dana: *Pull her access. All of it. It's better to go dark than to have her continue making a mess of things. I'll get you a statement today.*

"You said you came to Midwinter to disconnect," he said finally. "I thought that meant from noise. Not from people."

"I didn't want to bring it with me," she said. "I didn't want it to be the thing you saw first."

"It wasn't," he said quietly.

Then, "But when it showed up, you pulled away instead of toward me."

The words weren't harsh. They were careful. That almost made them worse.

Nora cleared her throat softly. "Maybe you two want a moment?" she said gently, and turned away to give them privacy.

Lila swallowed. "I wasn't hiding it to hurt you."

"I know," Evan said again. This time it meant something different.

He stared past her, eyes fixed on the window where sunlight hit the snow outside. When he looked back, his expression had shifted behind something more guarded.

"No," he said, voice lower now. "You were hiding because you didn't feel safe enough to stay open."

She nodded, tears burning. "Yes."

He rubbed a hand over his mouth, the motion weary more than angry. "And now?"

"I don't know," she whispered. "I didn't expect to find this here. I didn't expect..." Her voice broke. "I didn't expect to find you here."

That did it. Something in his face gave—not into softness, but into the kind of honesty that hurt.

He stepped closer, not enough to touch, but enough that she felt his heat. "Look at me," he said, very quietly.

She did.

His eyes searched hers, slow and steady, like he was checking for fractures. "Are you in trouble?" he asked. "The real kind. Not gossip."

"No," she breathed. "Just exposed."

He exhaled through his nose, a hard, controlled sound. "Okay."

He paid Nora, barely speaking, and guided Lila toward the door with a hand at the small of her back. The contact was brief and gentle, but it made her pulse jump like a guilty thing.

Outside, the cold hit hard.

In the truck, the silence arrived fast. The heater clicked on. The road stretched open and bright.

Lila tried to speak once, tried to explain, but the words died against the steady sound of the tires on packed snow.

Halfway up the mountain road, Evan's knuckles tightened on the steering wheel. "I thought we were meeting each other where we were," he said finally, eyes fixed ahead.

"I wanted that," she said. "I just didn't know how to let you see the part of me that was still ashamed."

His jaw flexed. "That's the part that scared me."

"You don't scare easily," she said.

"No," he agreed. "But I've learned what distance feels like when it starts."

Her throat burned. "I didn't lie."

"No," he said. "You closed a door."

The sentence landed with quiet finality.

They drove the rest of the way without speaking, the lodge appearing between pines like a place that could hold them—or fail to. Evan pulled in, parked, and sat there for a long moment, hands still on the wheel. His expression softened, but the distance remained, careful as a boundary.

"Thank you for coming," he said finally.

The politeness hurt more than anger would have.

She nodded, fingers tightening around her cup. "Evan..."

He looked at her, and for a second she thought he might reach across the console, might pull her in, might do something human and reckless.

Instead, he opened his door.

Cold air rushed in, sharp as glass. He stepped out and shut the door quietly behind him.

Lila sat there alone, staring at snow piled against the windshield. Her reflection wavered in the glass, pale and small.

The world she'd built here—quiet, safe, real—had cracked open.

She pressed her hand to her mouth to keep from sobbing, but the sound escaped anyway, muffled and raw.

Outside, Evan walked toward the lodge without looking back.

And for the first time since she'd arrived in Midwinter, Lila felt the cold reach her bones.

She didn't go inside right away.

Instead, she carried her coat and the untouched coffee up to the Lake Room and shut the door behind her. The room still smelled faintly of firewood and soap. Quiet waited where she'd left it—patient, but no longer neutral.

Her phone buzzed once in her pocket. Habit pulled at her hand, sharp and automatic. *Check. See what they're saying now.*

She didn't.

She set the phone facedown on the desk, slid it out of reach, and opened her notebook instead.

The page was blank. That helped.

She wrote slowly, not trying to sound brave or reasonable or worth forgiving. Just honest.

I didn't disappear because I was tired, she wrote. *I disappeared because I was afraid to stay and explain.*

She paused, pencil hovering, then kept going.

I let the noise get loud enough that I could justify leaving. I told myself silence would fix it. I told myself stepping away was the same as dealing with it.

It wasn't.

Her chest tightened, but she didn't stop. Writing steadied her in a way posting never had. There was no audience here. No comments waiting to decide what she meant. Just the truth arriving when it was ready.

I didn't fight back. I didn't clarify. I didn't stay and take the heat. I vanished and called it self-care.

The pencil pressed harder on the last word, the paper denting slightly.

I'm not proud of that. But I'm done pretending it didn't happen.

She set the pencil down and rested her palm over the page, feeling the faint indentation of the words. Her breathing slowed. The urge to justify herself out loud dulled, replaced by something steadier.

This wasn't for Evan. Not yet.

This was for the part of her that had gone quiet instead of answering back.

Outside, the lodge settled into evening. Somewhere below, a door opened and closed. Footsteps crossed the foyer. Life continued at its unbothered pace.

Lila stayed where she was, the notebook open in front of her, choosing words instead of silence for the first time in a long while.

Chapter 26

T he sound of the truck door closing followed him up the path. A single, clean thud, and then only the muffled crunch of his boots on the packed snow.

Evan didn't look back. He couldn't. The image of her sitting there, hands white around the coffee cup, eyes wide with something that wasn't quite guilt and wasn't quite fear, was already burned into him.

Inside, the lodge was too warm. The fire had been stoked high, the air heavy with pine and bread. He peeled off his gloves and coat, but the heat didn't reach past his skin.

He'd told himself not to care. From the start, he'd told himself she'd leave, that everyone did eventually. He'd built boundaries into the shape of his days. Repair the roof. Check the generator. Fix the loose latch on the pantry door. Work that stayed done. People never did.

And yet somewhere between her laugh on the sled hill and her hand on his wrist, he'd let the edges blur.

Ruth called from the kitchen. "You two get what you needed?"

Evan paused at the entryway. "Yeah," he said. "Road's clear. Café's fine."

"Good to hear." Her voice carried an unspoken question, and *Lila?* but she didn't ask.

He crossed the great room and stopped at the window. The truck still sat by the path, engine off, Lila's outline faint behind the frosted glass. She wasn't moving. Just sitting there, like someone who'd lost her place on a map.

He hated that he understood that feeling.

He turned away before she could see him watching.

The generator lights blinked steady on the panel. Green, green, green. He stared at them longer than necessary. Steady was good. Predictable was safe. He'd lived by those rules for years.

But lately, safety felt like another word for half-alive.

He thought of her voice at the café, small, breaking around the edges. *I didn't write those posts.* The tremor in her hand. The way her breath had hitched when she saw her own face on that rack, like the air had turned sharp.

She hadn't lied, not exactly. But omission was its own kind of betrayal.

He'd spent half his life covering for people who meant well and still left damage behind. His father's quiet temper. His brother's unfinished promises. Every time, he'd told himself understanding was the same as forgiveness.

It wasn't.

It was just another form of endurance.

Now here she was. Another person he'd let close. Another truth arriving late.

He rubbed a hand over his face and headed for the maintenance room. The smell of oil and metal steadied him. He flipped on the work light, the hum filling the silence, and started checking the emergency bins and counting headlamps.

Square the labels. Align the cans.

Anything to keep his hands busy so his chest didn't have to be.

The sound of the truck door finally reached him through the walls, a distant slam. Then the soft thud of footsteps on the porch.

He froze, fingers resting on a can of varnish.

He wanted her to walk past. Wanted her to come in. Wanted both, and hated himself for it.

He heard Ruth's voice again, gentle but uncertain. "Lila, sweetheart, you all right?"

A pause. A murmur too low to catch. Then the creak of floorboards as Ruth guided her toward the kitchen.

Evan's chest tightened. He replaced the can, turned off the light, and left through the side door.

The air outside bit at his face. He welcomed it. He walked the perimeter of the lodge, scanning the gutters for new cracks, pretending it was maintenance instead of escape. The sun had already slipped behind the ridge, and the first twilight shadows crawled up the snowbanks.

He reached the edge of the woods and stopped. Beyond the trees, the frozen lake gleamed under the fading light. It looked the same as it had that morning when she'd stood beside him, two people who had started to believe they could rebuild something out of silence.

Now that silence was all he had left.

He sat on the old bench near the treeline. The cold seeped through his jeans, grounding him. He tried to make sense of the tangle in his chest. Anger. Disappointment. And something deeper he didn't want to name because naming it made it real.

She hadn't meant to deceive him. He knew that. But he also knew what it felt like to trust the wrong version of someone, to believe the part they let you see, only to learn you were a background character in their real story.

He looked down at his hands. The skin across his knuckles was dry and cracked from the cold. He flexed his fingers, remembering the way she'd held them when she'd patched his wrist. How natural it had felt. How her thumb had hovered for a second too long, like she'd wanted to soothe more than the cut.

He'd let it happen.

That was on him.

A branch snapped behind him. He didn't move. A moment later, Ruth's quiet footsteps came through the snow.

"You planning to freeze out here?" she asked softly.

He gave a humorless laugh. "Working on it."

She came to stand beside the bench, pulling her shawl tighter. "She's in the kitchen. Said she needed water. Looks worse than you do."

"I'm not sure that's possible."

"She didn't say much. But I've seen that look before," Ruth said. "You don't have to explain."

"I don't think I could if I tried."

Ruth's gaze followed his toward the lake. "You know what I think? You two were bound to hit a truth sooner or later. That's all this is. Truths always hurt when they first arrive."

He rubbed his thumb along the edge of the bench. "She came here needing to disappear, Ruth. I get that."

Ruth stayed quiet.

"What I didn't get," he continued, voice lower now, "was realizing she'd been standing right beside me while keeping part of herself sealed off. Not because she didn't trust me—but because she didn't trust herself."

Ruth's expression softened.

"It's not the fear that bothers me," he said. "It's the distance. One day she was here with me. The next, it felt like I was reaching for someone who'd stepped back without saying a word."

Ruth gave him a long, kind look. "Then maybe now's when you find out if you still want to."

She left him with that, disappearing back toward the lodge.

Evan stayed until his breath fogged thick in front of him, until the cold bit into his fingers enough to numb them. Then he stood and made his way back.

Through the window, he could see movement. Lila pacing near the fire, one hand pressed to her chest as if trying to hold herself together. The other hand kept lifting her phone, then dropping it again like it was hot.

He didn't go in. Not yet.

Instead, he circled to the workshop, grabbed a stack of kindling, and carried it to the woodpile. The small labor helped. Every piece stacked neat, ordered, solid. When his mind wouldn't settle, he turned to the things that didn't ask questions.

By the time he reentered the lodge, the lights had dimmed for the evening. Ruth and Walter had gone upstairs.

Only Lila remained, sitting on the hearth with her knees drawn up, the fire painting her face in flickering amber. Her hair had slipped loose from whatever she'd done with it earlier, soft around her temples. She looked smaller in the firelight. Not fragile. Just... human.

She looked up when she heard his steps but didn't rise.

"I'll get out of your way," she said quickly.

"You're not in my way," he replied, and meant it.

Silence stretched between them, full and uneasy. The fire popped, and both of them flinched like the sound had done something personal.

She looked back at the flames. "I didn't expect anyone here to recognize me," she said quietly. "I thought if I disappeared long enough, it would stop mattering."

He leaned a shoulder against the wall, arms crossed because his hands needed a job. "You could've told me before it found you again."

"I know." Her voice broke. "I wanted to. Every time you looked at me like I was..." She swallowed hard. "Like I wasn't a headline."

His throat tightened. He didn't move. If he stepped closer, he wasn't sure he'd stop.

"It already has," he said, though softer than he meant.

She nodded, staring into the flames like the answer might be hidden in the coals. "I'm sorry."

He believed her. But believing her didn't erase the hollow ache under his ribs.

"I need some time," he said finally. "To think."

She nodded once. Her eyes shone, but the tears stayed where they were, controlled and stubborn. "Take all the time you need."

He turned to go, then stopped at the edge of the room. Not because he'd changed his mind, but because leaving felt like the first real punishment he'd ever handed her, and he didn't want that to be what this became.

He looked back. Her gaze flicked up, hopeful for a second before she schooled it away.

He didn't say what he wanted to say.

He only said the truest thing he could manage. "I'm not done."

Her breath caught, almost silent.

Neither of them moved.

Then he left before the moment asked for a touch he didn't trust himself to keep gentle.

Upstairs, the hallway lights were dim. The room smelled faintly of pine and ash. He sat on the edge of his bed and looked out the window toward the dark curve of the lake. The wind had shifted again, brushing snow from the roof in soft, steady drifts.

He thought of the morning they'd first met, the way she'd looked at the falling snow like it was mercy instead of burden. He thought of how easily she'd started to belong here, how quickly he'd wanted her to.

Now he wasn't sure what any of it meant.

Trust wasn't just honesty. It was consistency. It was showing up the same way, even when the world turned sideways.

He lay back, staring at the ceiling beams. The fire downstairs crackled faintly through the floorboards, and every pop of sap sounded like a memory burning.

He closed his eyes, but rest wouldn't come. Somewhere below, she was still awake. He could feel it, the same way he'd felt her presence long before either of them had said the right words out loud.

He didn't know what tomorrow would look like.

But he knew the simple truth that sat heavy and immovable inside him.

He still cared.

And that was the part he couldn't fix.

Chapter 27

The storm had returned overnight, not fierce, just enough to whisper against the windows. Snow drifted lazily past the glass, settling soft as dust along the porch rail. Inside Ember Lodge, the air carried a quiet that filled the cracks between words people weren't saying.

Lila spent most of the afternoon in the library nook pretending to read. Her laptop stayed shut on the table beside her, the black screen a kind of peace she didn't trust. Every so often she heard Evan moving through the hall, the measured tread of his boots, the faint scrape of his toolbox, the soft click of a latch being tested twice, then once more because he didn't believe in "probably fine."

Her heart twisted every time.

He didn't linger. He didn't seek her out. He didn't punish her with anger either, which was worse because anger was a door you could knock on. His restraint was space. Clean, careful space.

Ruth appeared in the doorway with a folded linen napkin in hand, as if she'd been summoned by the exact moment Lila started spiraling.

"Dear," Ruth said softly, "you've been hiding in here since breakfast. That's no food for the soul."

"I'm keeping out of the way," Lila said.

"You're not in the way." Ruth's kindness left no room for refusal. "I made a pot roast. Evan's been working out back. He won't eat unless I bribe him. Come help me carry dishes."

"Ruth, maybe it's better if—"

"Dinner's at six," Ruth said, smiling like she'd already won. "You can either help serve or sit awkwardly while Walter and I talk about the weather. Either way, you're eating."

When Ruth left, Lila exhaled and pressed her palms to her knees. She'd faced critics and comment sections at their worst, but the thought of sitting across from Evan made her stomach flutter like she'd broken something she couldn't fix.

She forced herself up anyway.

Because hiding was how she'd ended up here.

By the time she reached the dining room, lamps were turned low, the table set with simple white dishes and Ruth's heavy ceramic tureen. Thyme and baked bread warmed the air. Walter unfolded his napkin at the end of the table with all the ceremony of a man who believed dinner mattered.

Evan was already there, sleeves rolled, hair damp from melting snow. He looked up when she entered. Polite. Guarded. But he didn't look away.

"Hey," he said.

"Hi," she answered, soft enough that it didn't feel like a performance.

Ruth arrived with a basket of bread and the sort of bright cheer that held a room together. "Now, this looks almost like peace," she declared, setting the basket down. "Walter, no crossword until after you've eaten. Evan, sit. If you take another bite standing, I'm confiscating your toolbox."

Walter chuckled. Even Evan managed a small grin that didn't quite reach his eyes.

They passed bowls and ladles, motions careful and polite. Lila focused on the dinner, grateful for clinks of silverware and the steady fire. Every sentence felt like a thread she didn't trust to pull.

"So," Ruth said after a few minutes, pushing potatoes around with deliberate casualness, "Lila, how long do you plan to stay now that the roads are open?"

Lila's spoon paused midair. Her chest tightened. "I'm not sure yet."

"No rush," Ruth said. "Midwinter keeps people until they've learned what they came for."

Evan's spoon paused, too. He glanced at Ruth, then at Lila. "And what's that?"

Ruth's smile softened. "Usually themselves."

Silence fell again, softer this time, like air after snowfall. Soon Ruth and Walter excused themselves. Dishes to wash, chores to tend, a retreat so practiced it was practically a blessing.

When the kitchen door swung shut, two untouched mugs of coffee cooled between Lila and Evan.

"Ruth is subtle," Lila said, tracing the rim of her cup.

"She's patient," Evan replied. His tone was mild, but distance still lived in it.

"You don't have to sit here if it's uncomfortable."

"It's not that." He leaned back, folded his arms. "I don't know what to say yet."

"You don't owe me words."

"That's not true." He studied the coffee like it might offer instructions. "I've been thinking about what you said. About wanting to start over. I understand that more than you think. But disappearing doesn't erase what came before."

"I know." She kept her voice low. "I needed to breathe without being watched."

"And now?"

"Now I feel like I'm standing in two worlds and neither wants me." Her throat tightened. "And I don't know how to explain what happened without sounding like I'm asking you to excuse it."

Something gentler broke through his restraint. "You're not the only one who's tried to build something new from wreckage."

"You mean after—"

He shook his head. "Doesn't matter." Quiet finality. Then, slower: "What matters is, I don't do well with distance I don't understand."

She stilled.

"You didn't lie to me," he continued. "But you pulled away without letting me know why. And that's hard for me."

The words hit her like a hand held out in the dark.

Her breath caught. The fire crackled. The clock ticked.

He nodded and pushed his chair back, as if he needed the movement to keep from saying more. "You should rest. It's been a long few days."

Before she could answer, a sharp drip sounded from the hall, followed by another, then a thin patter like fingers on a drum.

Evan's head snapped toward the noise. "South eave," he said, already on his feet. "Ice backflow."

He moved for the mudroom. Lila stood, too. "What do you need?"

He hesitated only a beat. "Buckets, towels, and a steady pair of hands."

The corridor by the back stair had turned into a shining oval on the floor. Meltwater slid from a seam in the beadboard ceiling and spattered the braided runner.

Evan slid a bucket under the leak and tossed a towel across the worst of the spread. "Ruth had me cut a relief channel last storm," he said. "Must have bridged again. I can clear it from the eave."

"I'll help." Lila rolled up the runner and swapped the full towel for a dry one. "Tell me what to do."

"Grab the short ladder from the closet and the orange-handled scraper. I'll pull the exterior slush away. You watch the seam. If the drip changes pitch, tell me."

They worked without fuss. Lila steadied the ladder as he unlatched the narrow window over the stair landing and shouldered it open to the night. Cold slid in, bright and clean. He eased onto the small rooflet with the practiced care of someone who respected edges.

"Okay," he said, bracing. "Hand me the scraper."

She passed it up and held his wrist a second longer than necessary while he found his balance.

He didn't pull away.

For a beat, her gloved hand was around him, firm and careful. She could feel the heat under the wool, the pulse there, steady as his voice.

Snow whispered against shingles. He chipped a clean path above the gutter, then carved a thin channel through the pale ridge that trapped the melt. When slush finally sluiced outward with a wet sigh, the bucket's frantic patter softened to an occasional tap.

"Pitch changed," Lila called. "Good change."

"Copy." He cleared one more ridge, then tapped the gutter to ensure flow. "All right. Closing up."

He swung inside, boots careful on the ladder. Their breath fogged the air. They stood shoulder to shoulder, cheeks flushed, listening to the room settle. The bucket ticked once. Silence, the good kind, returned.

"Thank you," he said.

"You're welcome," she answered, and meant it for more than the ladder.

They sopped the damp, reset the runner, and left the bucket as insurance. The whole thing took ten minutes.

No drama. Just two people doing the ordinary thing correctly. The work felt like a language she could still speak.

At the mudroom, he peeled off wet gloves. Water darkened the cuff of his sleeve. He flexed his hand once, as if testing whether the world was still holding.

"You're steady," he said.

"I'm better with instructions."

His mouth tipped. "I'm good at practical."

"I know."

The line between them thinned. Not fixed. Not the old distance either.

She should have stepped back. Instead, she reached for his sleeve and brushed the wet fabric as if she could smooth the moment into place. "You're going to freeze like that."

He went still. His gaze dropped to her hand, then lifted to her face.

"Lila," he said quietly, like he was warning her and inviting her at the same time.

"I'm sorry," she said, and the words came out raw. "Not just for the café. For pulling away. For letting you think you were safe with me when I was still hiding."

His throat worked once. He didn't look away.

"I don't know if I can do this the way you want me to," she whispered. "But I can do it honest."

That did something to him. She saw it in the shift of his shoulders, the way his breath changed.

He stepped closer, not crowding, just closing the air. Warmth. Pine smoke. The faint soap scent of his jacket, familiar now in a way that made her chest hurt.

"Honest is the only way," he said.

"I know."

Her eyes flicked to his mouth and back, quick, like she'd been burned for wanting before.

His hand lifted, slow, giving her time to pull away. He touched her cheek with the back of his fingers, careful as if he were checking for a bruise.

Low heat. Not a claim. A question.

She leaned into it before she could overthink.

For a moment they just stood there, breath mingling, the lodge quiet around them like it was holding its own breath, too.

His thumb shifted, barely, at the corner of her jaw.

"Tell me to stop," he murmured.

The honesty in it unraveled her. "Don't."

He bent and kissed her, gentle at first, like he was testing the ice. Then a little deeper when she answered, when she tilted up and held on to the front of his jacket like she needed proof he was real.

Warm. Slow. Real.

When he pulled back, his forehead rested against hers. He exhaled, and his breath trembled like he'd been holding it for days.

"That," he said, voice rougher, "doesn't fix anything."

"I know," she whispered.

His hand slid from her cheek to her neck, thumb resting beneath her ear, a steady anchor. He didn't push. He didn't take more. He stayed there, letting the moment exist without demanding it turn into a promise.

Then, with effort, he stepped back. "Get some sleep," he said gently. "I'll walk the perimeter and call it a night."

She nodded, heart pounding. "Good night, Evan."

"Good night, Lila."

—

Later, in her room, the hush pressed closer. Snowlight pooled pale across the floor. Juniper claimed the pillow beside her, a warm comma.

Lila sat at the desk with a blank page and started writing before she could talk herself out of it.

Evan,

I should have told you everything the night we met. Not because I owed you a confession, but because you deserved to know what I was carrying. I was afraid of what that truth might change, of what you might see differently once the quiet broke.

I thought I could build a calmer version of myself here. Someone lighter. Someone not shaped by other people's expectations. But every time I stayed silent, every time I stepped back instead of toward you, I built a wall I didn't mean to build.

Tonight you didn't push. You didn't demand answers. You just stayed. You made space without leaving it empty, and that mattered more than I can say.

I'm sorry for pulling away instead of trusting you with the whole of me. For the distance I created because I wasn't sure honesty could be safe yet. That fear is mine to own.

I don't know what happens next. But I want to do this right. Not perfectly. Just honestly.

If you can't forgive me, I'll understand. But I don't want to disappear again.

— L.

She stared until the words blurred. The ink glistened under the lamp, as if waiting for permission to belong. Juniper pressed her head against Lila's wrist.

"I know," Lila whispered. "Not too late. Not if I stop running."

She folded the letter once, then again.

This time she didn't hide it in the drawer.

She slid it into an envelope and wrote his name on the front. She slipped it under his door, where he'd have to choose to take it. Where it would be consent, not intrusion.

The storm thickened outside, muting the pines and the lake beyond, as she returned to her room.

Down the hall, a floorboard creaked, then another. Evan's measured steps, making a last round.

She heard the pause outside her door. The quiet intake of breath. Then the soft, deliberate sound of paper being picked up.

No footsteps retreated fast. No slammed doors.

Just the slow continuation of the lodge settling, like it approved.

Lila turned down the lamp and let the storm say what words couldn't.

—

The storm deepened around midnight. Not wild, not loud. Snow tapped softly along the eaves, a patient sound. Ember Lodge answered with low creaks and settling beams, like it knew how to ride this out.

Evan stood in the hall with the envelope in his hand, her handwriting stark against the dim light.

He didn't open it right away.

He leaned his shoulder against the wall and stared at her door, at her name, as if it were something mechanical. Something he could fix if he just understood the angle.

After a moment, he slid a finger under the flap.

He read slowly. Once, all the way through. Then again, pausing only where the words stayed plain. No defenses. No polishing. Just truth, set down without asking for mercy.

Not perfect. Right.

He closed his eyes.

Years ago, he'd learned how hard it was to let someone see you without bracing for impact.

She was trying.

That counted.

He didn't knock. He didn't turn the night into a conversation that would demand more than either of them could give. He carried the letter downstairs instead, fed the hearth two pieces of kindling, and watched the embers take. Warmth touched his face, brief and honest.

When he returned to the hall, he set the empty envelope on the table beneath the lamp. Beside it, he left the small metal key he kept on his ring, the one for the storage room with the extra blankets and the good lantern.

On the back of the tag, he wrote a single line.

Don't disappear. Knock.

He left it there and went on with his rounds.

Outside, snow gathered at the window, steady and unthreatening. The lodge held its warmth. The night did what nights did.

For the first time in days, the storm felt like it was loosening its grip.

Chapter 28

L ila woke to the pale, pearly light that meant the clouds had settled low over the lake. The bedroom smelled like cedar and clean wool. The lodge's old radiator ticked in the corner, a familiar metronome that had kept time through long nights she had not expected to spend here.

Frost ringed the window like lace. Somewhere down the hall, a floorboard sighed. Juniper trilled once in the corridor, a queen making her rounds.

Lila reached for her phone on the nightstand and stared at the dark screen.

No alerts. No new messages from the world she had once trained herself to serve within minutes.

She turned the phone over in her hands. The weight felt heavier today. Decision had a way of doing that.

The flight confirmation sat in her email on the lodge computer like a sealed envelope.

She didn't need to open it again to know what it said.

She had booked it after midnight when sleep wouldn't come and her thoughts kept running the same loop: stay and risk hurting him, or leave and hurt him in a way that felt cleaner. She had crept to the little office off the lobby where the router sat next to a basket of peppermint tea. The connection had flickered in and out, stubborn as a mule. Still, she had managed to secure an early seat on the morning run to the city and then onward to Denver.

Leaving meant relief. That was what she'd told herself in the dark.

Relief from the humiliation of the confrontation. Relief from the way Evan had gone so still after, like a man who had watched a bridge he trusted give way under his boots. Relief from Ruth's gentle eyes.

From her own need.

Now, in the half-light, relief felt like an empty suitcase. It would carry what she packed. It would still be hollow.

She dressed in soft layers. Thermal top. A blue sweater. Jeans. Two pairs of socks. She folded the sweater's cuffs back over her wrists and listened to the quiet. Snow hadn't started yet. The lake was a sheet of dull pewter beyond the glass. If she held very still, she could hear the whisper of wind finding the eaves.

She opened her suitcase on the bed and began to gather the life she had poured into the room.

Camera lens wrapped in a scarf. Notebook with its soft leather cover. The pen she'd started to favor because it scratched just enough. The pile of postcards she had never written, each one a small winter scene that didn't need her words to be complete. Her boots thumped the floor when she lifted them.

Then her gaze landed on the letter.

Three pages, folded once, edges sharp. She had written it last night after the leak, after the way Evan had kissed her like truth and then stepped back like he was afraid of what truth could cost.

She touched the letter's corner with one finger. She tried to imagine the sound it would make if she slid it into his hands. A whisper. A last try.

She pictured him reading it at the counter in that worn flannel, head bent, the crease forming above his nose when he was hurt, not angry.

Would it matter? Would truth, late and clumsy, ever be enough?

She slid the letter into the side pocket of her duffel and zipped it closed before she could change her mind.

In the corridor, Juniper sat like a gray stone in the path and watched her with large, unbothered eyes.

"I know," Lila whispered. "I'm not the first to leave."

Juniper blinked and rose with a swish of her tail, then led the way down the stairs as if escorting a guest of state.

The lobby was warm. Lamps glowed in corners the way stars gather near a horizon. The big stone fireplace was a bed of ash with a handful of embers still pulsing.

Lila paused to feed the fire. She knew the rhythm now. Kindling first. Then a split log pushed into the heart. Wait for the flame to catch.

The crackle landed in her chest like breath she had been holding too long.

She brushed her hands and stood. The day waited.

Ruth was already at the desk with a ledger open. She looked up and smiled the way some people pray, with their whole face.

"Morning, honey."

"Morning." Lila's voice worked on the second try. "I booked a flight. The early one."

Ruth nodded like she had expected that answer and had already done the math. "The plows came through after dawn. Roads should stay clear until midday."

Lila exhaled. She hadn't realized how tightly she'd been holding that breath.

"Walter can help you load up," Ruth added. "And he'll insist on directions you don't need and advice you didn't ask for."

The joke landed with a soft thud that wasn't unkind. Lila's mouth curved even as her throat tightened. "Thank you."

Ruth came around the desk and set a hand on Lila's arm. Warm. Steady. "It has been a gift having you here."

"I made it complicated," Lila said. The words came out small.

"Complicated is just a look at what we care about," Ruth replied. "It means there was something to lose."

Lila swallowed. The lamps hummed. Somewhere, Walter coughed awake, a bear in a den.

"Is he around?"

Ruth's gaze flicked past Lila to the hallway that led to the utility room. "He's been outside since first light. Checking roofs. He does that when his head is loud." She squeezed gently. "You don't have to fix him. You don't have to fix this before you go."

"I'd like to try," Lila said. "But I don't know how."

"Sometimes we don't have to know," Ruth said. "Sometimes we tell the truth, and it sits where it needs to sit until the person it's for is ready to pick it up. You have told it. That matters."

Her mouth twitched. "And sometimes a person needs to carry wood until his arms shake before he can hear anything at all."

The image was so exactly Evan that Lila almost laughed. The sound snagged and turned into air.

"I'll be in the kitchen," Lila said. "I want to make coffee for the road."

"You sit," Ruth said. "I already packed you up." She nodded to the counter, where a paper sack waited beside a travel mug. The mug wore a knitted sleeve in cranberry red.

"Cinnamon rolls. Two. One for now and one for when the grief hits and you think about turning around."

"You keep making it very hard to go."

"That's because I'm not in the business of goodbye," Ruth said. "I'm in the business of see you soon."

Lila lifted the sack and held it to her chest for a moment as if it were as fragile as a bird. Then she turned toward the lake window. The view gathered itself as more light pooled. The ice looked heavier today. The line of trees on the far shore wore a stillness that pressed against the glass.

Her reflection wavered within it.

For a second she could almost believe she belonged on both sides.

Then Walter's boots thudded down the back stairs, and the spell let her go.

They carried her suitcase and duffel out to the porch. Her rental sat at the edge of the drive, dusted with frost like sugar, its windshield clouded white in the early light.

Walter set her suitcase in the back and closed the hatch with a gentle thump.

"Bennie called," he said. "Main road is clear to the highway. It will get slick near the bridge after the turn, so mind your speed."

"I will." She hesitated, then added, "Thank you for seeing me off."

"You kept Ruth company during the long watch," Walter said. "That is more than a fair trade."

Lila nodded, throat tight, and looked past him toward the shed. The door stood ajar. She could see the neat edge of stacked wood inside.

Her heart found a rhythm and then stumbled.

Evan stepped out from the shadow.

Coil of rope over one shoulder. Glove tucked under his belt. Flannel open at the throat, collar turned up against the cold. He saw Walter first. Then Ruth. Then her.

The air thinned. Everything got quiet in a new way, as if even the trees leaned in.

"Morning," he said.

The word sat flat between them, but his eyes weren't.

"Morning," she answered.

His gaze moved, quick and controlled: her SUV, the open hatch, the suitcase. Then her face. She saw the question rise behind his eyes and settle into his jaw, where he wouldn't show it.

He crossed the yard and took the duffel from her hand. "I'll get that."

His palm brushed hers.

Heat. Even through gloves.

He set the bag in the back. He didn't look up, like looking up might crack something he was holding together by force.

Lila wanted to say everything at once. Not the letter. Not the careful draft. The mess behind her ribs.

I didn't tell you the first night because I didn't know how to be honest and safe at the same time. I liked who I was when you didn't know me. I wanted to be a person here. Not a headline.

"Juniper's going to miss your lap," Evan said.

She startled, then nodded. "She pretends otherwise."

"She pretends otherwise with everyone," he said, and there was almost warmth in it. Almost.

He reached to close the hatch. The sound of metal was too loud in the cold air.

Ruth moved with tact. "Walter, can you check the de-icer in the shed? The blue bottle. I think it wandered."

Walter understood. He always did. He gave Lila a hug and then headed toward the shed.

Ruth drifted back toward the porch. "I need to pull today's rolls out," she announced to no one, then disappeared inside.

The yard held only the two of them and thin winter air. Lila's breath rose and faded. Evan's hands rested on the edge of the hatch like he needed the anchor.

"I booked the first flight," Lila said. "I wasn't sure I should wait."

He nodded once. Then again. "That's probably smart."

She hated that word from his mouth. Smart belonged to decisions that had nothing to do with hearts.

"Ruth has my address," she said, trying for light and missing. "If you ever need to mail my dignity back."

He huffed. Almost a laugh. It frayed and vanished. "You didn't owe me anything."

"I owe you an explanation," she said. "I owed you that from the start."

He didn't move his hands. He didn't look at her. "You owed yourself kindness."

"I didn't know how to give it," she said. "Not with this. Not with the mistakes I made." Her voice shook. "I know it sounds like an excuse, but it's the only truth I have."

Evan closed his eyes. The lines at the corners deepened, making him look older and somehow more himself.

He was quiet for a moment, jaw working like he was deciding what deserved air.

"I don't like finding out after the fact," he said. "That I stepped into something without knowing the shape of it."

"I wasn't hiding from you," she said quickly. She stepped closer without meaning to. Cold filled the small space between them. "I was trying to protect a part of myself I didn't know how to explain yet."

He looked at her then. Really looked.

"I believe you," he said. And it still hurt.

The winter light in his eyes did something to her chest.

"It felt like it," he said. "It still does."

She nodded because she couldn't argue with a feeling. "I can't erase that. I can only stop adding to it."

A jay scolded from the fence post, sharp and bright. The moment shifted, like a fire when someone opens a window.

"I wrote you a letter," she said. "I didn't give it to you because I kept thinking I might earn the right to say it out loud."

His gaze flicked to the open hatch. Back to her face.

"Words don't rewind time," he said, then paused. "I mean—wanting to explain doesn't change how something lands."

"I know," she whispered. "That's why I didn't hand you paper like it was a solution."

She drew a breath that hurt. "But I want you to know something before I go."

He stayed still, shoulders tightening like he was bracing for weather.

"I didn't come here to hide from you," she said. "I came because I was empty. And when you looked at me like I mattered, I didn't know how to hold that and still protect myself." She swallowed. "What I felt was real. Even if I wasn't ready for all of it."

Something shifted in his face. Not forgiveness. Not yet. Recognition.

He took a slow breath. "I didn't tell you something either."

Her heart stuttered. "What?"

"I liked who I was with you," he said. Simple. Honest. Devastating in its quiet. "I haven't liked that man for a long time. I thought he was only good for fixing what other people broke."

His mouth pulled, like the confession embarrassed him.

"Then you asked me about the grain of a board. About the light on the lake at four in the afternoon." His voice roughened. "You laughed at Walter's terrible jokes. You looked at this place like it mattered. You made me feel like I wasn't only what I lost."

Her eyes burned.

"So I'm not very good at letting that happen," he finished.

The lake gave a soft, distant pop. Lila felt it in her bones.

"Evan—"

He shook his head. "You don't have to explain." Gentle. And it made everything worse. "You're leaving."

"I am," she said. The words tasted like iron. "I don't know if it's right. It's the only thing I know how to do without making it worse."

He nodded once, slower. "Then it's the right thing for now."

She stood there, wanting to touch him. Wanting to be touched. Wanting something that didn't come with consequences.

Evan lifted his hand like he meant to do the same.

He stopped himself.

Instead, he stepped in and adjusted the scarf Ruth had given her, tugging it snug at her throat. His knuckles brushed the bare skin at her collar.

A small, intimate touch that was also practical.

His breath warmed her for one second.

Her body reacted anyway, sharp and uninvited.

"Airport air will chew you up," he murmured, eyes on the scarf, not her mouth. "Keep it tight."

"Okay," she whispered.

He let his hand fall. Stepped back like distance was the only self-control he trusted.

The back door opened. Walter emerged with the blue bottle held high. "Found it."

Ruth followed, her eyes gentle and knowing. She hugged Lila, brief but firm. "For airport air."

"Thank you," Lila said.

"Drive careful," Ruth added. The kind of phrase that meant be safe without saying goodbye.

Lila climbed into her car. Cinnamon, coffee, old engine heat. She started it and let it idle.

Evan stepped back from the hatch. Rope on his shoulder. Glove in hand. A man holding himself together with habit.

She rolled the window down a few inches. Cold rushed in, stinging her eyes.

"I'm sorry," she said.

Evan met her gaze, steady as a nailed board. "I know," he said. "I am, too."

"For what?"

"For how I close doors when I feel something worth keeping," he said. He swallowed. "It keeps the heat in."

"It keeps a person alone," she said softly.

"Yeah."

Something eased. Not gone. Loosened.

She nodded. He nodded back. A pact. Or a blessing.

She eased the car down the drive. Snow crunched. She kept the window cracked and held on to the cold like it might keep her clear.

At the end of the lane, flakes began to fall. Big, slow coins of white. She turned onto the main road and watched the lodge recede in the mirror.

The porch rails. The chimney. A gray cat on the steps.

A man in flannel with his hands in his pockets, looking up.

She didn't cry. Not yet.

She stayed there. In the car. In the ache. Letting it be clean.

When the trees swallowed the last glimpse of roofline, she rested her forehead against her knuckles and told herself the only sentence she could survive right now:

Going didn't have to mean gone.

The road carried her forward. Snow kept falling.

And somewhere behind her, in a lodge that had been more than a hiding place, a man with rope on his shoulder would keep checking seams, listening for the shift in weight that tells you when something needs care.

Not because he could fix everything.

Because now he remembered what it felt like to want to try.

Chapter 29

Evan stayed where he was long after her car disappeared around the bend. The sound of the engine faded, swallowed by the hush that always came before new snow. The flakes had thickened—big, slow spirals drifting down like something trying to soften the world.

He stood on the porch with his hands shoved deep in his pockets, the cold needling his face, eyes fixed on the faint tracks she'd left through the white. They wouldn't last. Snow was already settling in, erasing them the way wind smoothed old footprints on the frozen lake.

He told himself he should go back inside. There was work waiting. There always was.

Instead, he lingered.

The yard felt emptier than it had any right to. Not the kind of absence made by sound leaving a space, but something heavier—as if a solid thing had been lifted away and the ground hadn't yet learned how to hold itself up.

Juniper brushed against his leg, then sat squarely at his boot, tail wrapped neat around her paws. She stared down the road, too, as if stubbornness alone might summon a return.

"Yeah," he said quietly. "I know."

She blinked once, unimpressed. Cats never mourned out loud.

Evan turned toward the lodge. Warm light glowed through the windows, making the snow on the panes shimmer gold. Ruth's silhouette moved in the kitchen, slow and deliberate, the way she always moved when she was thinking. Walter's hat hung on the peg by the door. Everything in its place.

Everything, except what wasn't.

He went to the shed and started splitting wood. The rhythmic crack of the axe became a kind of penance, the closest thing he knew to prayer. Each swing drove heat into his arms and pushed thought back, at least until he caught himself glancing toward the drive again, half-expecting her to reappear, breathless, saying she'd changed her mind.

She wouldn't.

She'd meant what she said—that she didn't know how to stay without making things harder. And he'd believed her, even as it cut.

He'd gone quiet when it mattered. Not to punish her. To protect himself.

He could still see her standing there, hands clenched at her sides, breath caught like she was holding something fragile inside. She'd started to speak once—really speak—and then stopped.

He knew that pause. The moment when a person understands that telling the whole truth might change the shape of a room forever.

She'd chosen silence. Not to deceive him. To survive the moment without losing herself.

His throat tightened anyway.

Because he had felt what that silence cost.

The shift in his own chest—from curiosity to care, from care to something that wanted roots. He didn't like wanting. Wanting meant letting someone else matter. Wanting meant risk.

The axe came down again, splitting a log clean. The sound cracked sharp, then softened under falling snow.

He stacked the pieces with the same care he brought to everything else. Neat rows. Tight corners. A wall of order against the parts of him that wanted to scatter.

When his arms began to burn, he stopped. He leaned the axe against the block and flexed his fingers until feeling returned.

Through the shed door, the lodge windows glowed. Warm. Steady. Safe.

Inside that safety was Ruth, who'd seen enough winters to know the difference between a person who needed quiet and a person who was hiding inside it.

He walked back toward the porch, snow collecting on his shoulders. Juniper followed at a dignified distance.

The moment he stepped inside, heat wrapped him like a blanket he hadn't earned. The lodge smelled like yeast and woodsmoke and lemon cleaner. Ordinary. Comforting.

Ruth stood at the counter with flour on her hands and a look that said she'd been listening for his boots.

"You done wearing yourself out?" she asked.

"Just splitting wood," Evan said, shrugging out of his coat.

"For an hour."

He didn't answer.

Ruth wiped her hands on a towel and set it aside. "Walter said you barely spoke when she pulled out."

"I didn't have much to say."

"That's not true," Ruth said gently. "You've got plenty to say. You just don't like how it feels when it's said out loud."

Evan stared at the floorboards. "I don't like not knowing where I stand."

"She didn't know either," Ruth said. "That's the part you're skipping."

He exhaled slowly. She was right. He'd offered her space like it was generosity, when half the time it had been armor. He'd let silence do the work and then wondered why it hurt.

"She left anyway," he said.

"She left because she thinks staying costs people something," Ruth said. "Because the last life she lived taught her that the moment you show a crack, someone tries to use it."

Evan looked toward the hallway, as if he could still see her moving there. Careful. Trying. So quiet it had nearly fooled him into thinking she was fine.

Ruth's voice softened. "You want to know what she did before she packed?"

He didn't trust himself to speak.

"She fed the fire," Ruth said. "Like it mattered whether the lodge stayed warm after she was gone."

Evan swallowed.

"And she asked if you were outside," Ruth added.

Ruth watched him, patient. "You can sit in it, or you can do one small thing that's true."

He stared at her. "I don't know how to fix it."

Ruth's mouth softened. "Then don't fix it. Just show up. The honest way."

Evan nodded once.

Not agreement. Decision.

He went down the hall to the small office off the lobby. The router lights blinked steady. The desk computer hummed when he woke it. He stood there a moment, hands on the chair back, breathing through the old instinct to do nothing.

Then he sat.

He didn't have her number. He'd never asked. Another quiet boundary he'd told himself was respect.

But he knew where the noise lived.

He opened a browser and typed her name. The page hung, loading in fits, like the lodge itself didn't want to invite the world back in. People talking like certainty was a game and consequences belonged to someone else.

His jaw tightened.

He scrolled until he found it—the same accusation repeated enough times it had started to look like fact. A comment thread spiraling into cruelty.

He could keep reading. Let it burn itself out.

Instead, he clicked reply.

He typed slowly. No rhetoric. No defense that spoke over her. Just the truth as he knew it.

I was with her when she found out. She was shaken. She said she didn't authorize those posts. Maybe don't convict real people on rumor.

He paused, reread it, then added one last line.

You don't get to turn someone's life into entertainment because it's easier than waiting for facts.

He hit post.

The words appeared on the screen. Plain. Unadorned. Attached to his name.

He didn't stay to argue. Didn't refresh to see what came back. He closed the browser and shut the computer down.

Outside, snow kept falling. Inside, the lodge hummed and breathed and went on.

He walked back toward the kitchen, where Ruth stood like she'd known he would choose something.

"What did you do?" she asked.

Evan exhaled. "I told the truth," he said. "Once. Where it mattered."

Ruth nodded. "Good."

She slid a plate toward him. "Now eat something before you pass out and we have to drag you through the snow like a sack of potatoes."

Evan almost smiled.

Almost.

Because under the hurt, under the fear, one truth held steady:

He wasn't ready for her to be gone.

And if the story was going to end well, he was going to have to stop acting like wanting was the first step toward losing.

Chapter 30

T he world outside the airport window was the same
gray she had left behind, only louder. Engines
hummed. Announcements cracked through tinny speak-
ers. People hurried past with coffee and phones like they
knew exactly where they were going.

Lila sat in a row of molded chairs, her coat folded
across her lap, the taste of a cinnamon roll still faint on
her tongue. The plane she'd meant to board had already
pushed back. She'd watched it taxi, snow swirling over its
wings, until it disappeared into white.

She wasn't sure why she hadn't stood when they called
her group. She'd held the ticket. She'd even risen halfway.
When the final boarding call sounded, her body stayed
rooted. Not fear. Not indecision. Something quieter, like
her pulse had found a rhythm the room couldn't hear.

She looked down at the paper ticket in her hand. A
melted snowflake had blurred the corner. Denver. Gate 12.

A clean path back to noise. Back to deadlines and meetings and an inbox full of people who hadn't noticed she was gone.

Maybe that was the problem.

Her phone buzzed. An unread email preview lit the screen—*Following up on our earlier message.*

She turned the screen facedown. In the dark glass, her reflection looked tired. Older. Not polished. Just her. The woman she used to be would have posted something already.

#LeavingMidwinter. #BackToRealLife. This version of her didn't want the old life back unless she could change what counted.

She had come to see if quiet could hold her.

It had.

A toddler laughed down the concourse. A man coughed into a paper cup. People moved with purpose. She stayed still. Could she go back to performing? To filters and captions. The question dropped into her chest and didn't echo.

She thought of Ember Lodge. Firelight turning walls to gold. The smell of pine and coffee. Juniper thudding into her lap like a small, deliberate weight. Ruth's patient wisdom. Walter's dry humor. Evan's steady hands. The way he watched the lake as if the light there might answer something worth asking.

Her throat tightened, but the feeling didn't unseat her.

She tore the ticket in half. The sound was soft. Final.

When she stood, her legs trembled. Not nerves. Clarity.

She passed the gate without looking back. Outside, snow kept falling in a patient drift, as if it were waiting for her to match its pace. At the rental counter, the clerk slid a form across. The pass north was open, according to the DOT alert taped to the screen. Chains recommended after mile marker fifty-two.

She signed, took the keys, and stepped into the swirl of white.

Cold cut her cheeks. The first breath hit her lungs like truth. For the first time in a long while, she didn't need to prove she felt it. She only had to feel it.

She drove north.

Not to chase someone. Not to outrun a headline. She drove toward the only place that had made the noise make sense.

The highway narrowed and climbed. Plows had cleared a clean center lane and thrown low ridges of snow to either side. Pines rose along the shoulders, their dark limbs holding the quiet in place. The pass held. She kept a steady speed and let the miles settle her.

Chapter 31

It wasn't until now, with only the wind and the smell of cedar for company, that Evan admitted it hadn't been anger keeping him shut off.

It was fear. Plain, stupid fear.

He'd spent years making his life small on purpose. Work. The lodge. The Mercers. Routine. He'd told himself solitude was cleaner than loss. Easier than waking up one day and realizing you'd started needing someone again.

Then Lila arrived and made a mess of his clean order.

She'd come in like winter sun, too bright to stare at for long. And somehow he'd stared anyway. He'd let her into the edges of his days. He'd liked the sound of her moving through the halls, the way she filled quiet without breaking it.

And then the moment in town.

The pause at the counter.

The sideways looks.

That soft, almost-kind question asked too carefully to be harmless.

Is it true?

Not shouted. Not chased. Just *known enough to be repeated.*

The realization hit harder than spectacle ever could. The woman he'd let into his calm carried a story that didn't belong to this place, one people felt entitled to pick at. Not because she was famous. Because she was *interesting*. And interesting things in small towns never stayed private for long.

He'd told himself he didn't judge her. That he just needed time.

What he'd really done was punish her for a life he didn't understand. For making him feel like an outsider in his own story.

The axe bit deep into the log. The wood split clean, a neat fault line that didn't argue.

He set the axe down and didn't pick it up again.

"I don't know how to do easy," he said aloud, to no one and to her all at once. "And I don't know how to promise things I haven't earned."

The words sat in the cold air, honest and unadorned.

"But I know this," he added quietly. "I don't want this to be temporary."

He exhaled, breath fogging.

"If she comes back, I'll stay. Not careful. Not halfway. I know how to stay."

Snow gathered on the pile beside him, softening the edges. He wiped his wrist across his forehead and felt the sting of cold on the scrape she'd cleaned. He could still remember the heat of her fingers when she'd wrapped his hand, the way she'd held him steady like he was worth care.

That was the problem.

You didn't forget someone like that.

He'd thought she'd fade. People left Midwinter all the time. You learned to watch taillights vanish and not build a life around the gap.

But Lila hadn't been a taillight. She'd been a presence. Small things that stayed: the extra mug by the sink, her crooked grocery lists, the way she hummed when she thought she was alone. The way she'd stood beside him at the window and made the space between them feel possible.

You couldn't unmake that. You just lived with the echo.

He stacked the last of the wood and went inside.

Warmth hit him like a hand at the back of his neck. Ruth's stew scented the air, thick with thyme and onions. Juniper streaked past his boots toward the kitchen like she'd been given a job to do.

"You'll freeze yourself out there," Ruth said, towel in hand. "Soup's on. Sit."

He wasn't hungry. But no one refused Ruth twice.

He dropped onto the bench by the fire. Ruth set a full bowl in front of him.

"You're thinking too hard for a man with soup," she said.

"I'm fine."

She tapped her spoon once against the rim. "People only say that when they're trying not to feel what's already chewing on them."

He let out a short laugh before he could stop it. The sound surprised him with its relief.

"She shouldn't have had to leave like that," he said.

"No," Ruth agreed. "But sometimes leaving is the only way a person knows how to stop the bleeding."

He stared into the stew. "I made it harder than it needed to be."

"You made it human," Ruth said. "That's about as honest as people get."

"She didn't deserve how I pulled back."

"No," Ruth said gently. "And you don't deserve the hurt that taught you to shut doors before someone else can."

He swallowed. "Do you think she'll come back?"

Ruth met his eyes. No soft lies. "Maybe. But only if she believes you won't punish her for being complicated. And only if you stop hiding behind pride."

The words landed clean.

After lunch, the lodge shifted into its quiet rhythm. Ruth vacuumed the guest wing. Walter worked on a hinge down the hall.

Evan stood in the doorway of Lila's old room. The bed was made. The air held that careful emptiness a space gets right after someone leaves. He told himself he was only there to check the window latch.

His boot nudged something under the dresser.

He crouched and pulled out a small bundle of envelopes tied with twine.

They weren't all for him.

To Me.

To the Girl I Used to Be.

To Whoever Still Believes in Quiet Things.

His throat tightened.

He opened the top one. The handwriting was careful but unsteady.

I came here to hide, but the quiet doesn't let you hide. It makes you listen. I thought I lost myself in what people expected me to be. Maybe I was lonely. Maybe I kept telling stories to strangers because I didn't know how to tell the truth up close. I want to learn how. I want to live slower, even if the world forgets me for it.

The room seemed to breathe.

Anger drained away, leaving something simpler. She hadn't come to escape success. She'd come to escape loneliness.

He hadn't been ready to hear it.

Ruth appeared in the doorway. "You found what she left."

"She wasn't pretending," he said. "She was tired."

Ruth nodded. "Aren't we all."

When she left, the quiet felt kinder.

Evan set the letters on the nightstand and watched the snow drift past the window. Somewhere beyond the ridge, a car would be climbing, tires whispering through fresh powder. He didn't know if Lila was behind the wheel.

He wouldn't decide that story before it arrived.

He turned off the lamp and closed the door. The lodge didn't feel empty.

Neither did he.

Not healed.

But honest.

And for the first time in a long while, honesty felt like a beginning instead of a loss.

Chapter 32

When Lila stepped into the foyer, warmth rose to meet the cold still caught in her coat. It pressed against her skin, gentle but insistent, like the lodge was reminding her it knew how to hold things steady. The lamp by the stairs threw a soft circle on the floor, familiar and unchanged, and for a split second her chest tightened with the fear that she had imagined all of it.

Ruth looked up from the desk. Surprise flared, sharp and bright, then settled into relief as natural as breath.

"Roads were good," Lila said. Her voice came out rough, scraped thin by cold and distance and the long drive back through her own thoughts.

"They were waiting," Ruth said. "We all were."

The words landed deeper than Lila expected. Waiting implied space had been left. That no one had moved on from her absence as if it were a relief.

Her boots left small puddles on the hummingbird rug. Her hands were stiff around the strap of her bag, fingers trembling now that the drive was done. She hadn't realized how cold she'd been until the warmth hit her all at once.

Ruth crossed the lobby with purpose. "Shower. Now. Before you freeze where you stand."

Lila nodded, throat tight, and made her way down the hall. The guest wing greeted her with its familiar creaks and lemon-oil hush. Her room glowed with soft lamplight, warm as a held breath. Everything was exactly where she'd left it that morning: the borrowed sweater on the hook, the quilt pulled tight, slippers tucked neatly beside the bed like they'd been guarding the space.

The sight of it stole her breath.

She turned the shower on as hot as it would go. When the steam rose, she stepped in and let the water crash over her. The heat hit hard enough to make her gasp. She braced her hands against the tile and stayed there while the cold broke apart in her muscles and drained away.

In the rush of heat, the truth finally settled.

She hadn't wanted to leave.

Not the quiet. Not the people. Not the version of herself she'd found tucked between snowstorms and mornings by the fire.

And not Evan.

When she stepped out, her skin was flushed, her hair clinging in dark waves around her shoulders. She dressed slowly in soft leggings and thick socks, then pulled on the blue sweater Ruth had insisted she borrow when she'd first arrived. It was warm from the vent, and it still smelled faintly of cedar.

A small, shaky laugh escaped her. She'd come back. She'd actually come back.

Downstairs, voices drifted up the stairwell. Walter's low baritone. Ruth's steady cadence. The clatter of dishes. It wrapped around her like a blanket.

When she stepped into the lobby, Ruth looked up from setting mugs on a tray. There was no surprise now. Just recognition.

"There you are," Ruth said. "Sit before the heat drifts past you."

Walter appeared with a folded blanket and draped it over the back of Lila's chair. "Storm's chewing at the ridge," he said. "You timed your return just right."

Lila wrapped her hands around the mug Ruth pressed into them. Cinnamon and honey lifted into the air. The heat seeped into her palms, then deeper.

The back hallway door creaked.

She didn't turn at first. Her heartbeat stumbled anyway.

Evan stepped into the room, glove in one hand, hat in the other. Sawdust dusted his hair. He didn't move. He just looked at her.

There was no anger in his face. No distance.

Only something bruised, and careful, and open in a way that made her chest ache.

"You came back," he said.

No question. Just a fact he was letting himself believe.

"I did."

She waited for the urge to explain. To justify. It didn't rise. The drive back had burned that urgency out of her mile by mile.

He glanced at the pink at her knuckles, the damp hem of her jeans. "Do you need tea," he asked, "or ten quiet minutes?"

The question loosened something in her chest. Not because he was asking. Because he wasn't assuming.

"Yes," she said, and almost smiled.

Ruth vanished toward the kitchen with the sound of a kettle and a plan. Walter retreated to his crossword with exaggerated discretion.

Lila and Evan stood near the stairs. Snow glittered on the porch where she'd carried it in on her boots. The air smelled of woodsmoke and lemon oil and something baked earlier that still lingered like a promise.

"I found some letters," he said, careful. "Some were to you."

She nodded. No flinch. "I was trying to tell the truth somewhere."

"You did."

The certainty in his voice surprised her. He wasn't handing the words back like evidence. He wasn't asking for explanations. He'd heard them for what they were.

"Tomorrow," he said, "if the wind stays down, the ice will catch the light near the middle. Nine o'clock."

"I know the place."

"Good."

Dinner unfolded without ceremony. Chicken, bread, warmth passed hand to hand. Lila ate because she was told to, because comfort felt like medicine. Every few minutes her gaze tugged toward Evan, toward the way he kept checking she was still there.

Afterward, she sat by the fire with another mug of tea, toes thawing, hair drying in soft waves. Snow whispered against the windows.

She let herself admit the truth she'd been holding since the airport.

She'd turned back for herself. For the quiet. For the chance to stop running.

But she'd also turned back because she couldn't stomach leaving this warmth behind.

A floorboard creaked behind her.

Evan didn't come closer. He leaned against the wall, close enough she could feel his presence like a shift in weather.

"You warm enough?" he asked.

"Getting there."

"Good."

She breathed out slow, the knot in her chest easing at last.

She didn't know what tomorrow would ask of her. She didn't know what they were yet.

But this moment was steady. Warm. Honest.

For now, it was enough.

Chapter 33

E van lingered near the edge of the lobby long after dinner plates were carried to the kitchen. He worked his thumbs along the seam of his flannel pocket in small, absent motions, pretending he was listening to Walter and Ruth bicker about the correct ratio of flour to butter in roux. He wasn't. His attention kept drifting—to the arm-chair near the fire, to the soft halo of lamplight pooling around Lila as she warmed her fingers around her mug.

She looked smaller than she had that morning when she'd left. Not fragile. Just... worn. The way people looked after they'd tried to be strong for too long and finally let themselves stop bracing.

He hadn't realized he'd been holding his own breath until she returned. She was here.

He still wasn't entirely sure what to do with that.

He waited until Ruth disappeared into the kitchen with a purposeful clatter and Walter excused himself to the back hall for "evening rounds," which Evan suspected was code for giving them a minute. The lodge quieted around him. Fire snapped. Snow whispered against the porch. The world felt small in the good way—held rather than closed in.

Lila shifted in her chair, pulling the blanket Ruth had left over her lap. The motion made a loose curl of her hair slide forward across her cheek. She pushed it back absently.

He didn't move toward her yet. His feet stayed planted near the entry table, as if crossing the room required permissions he hadn't earned.

He wasn't used to this kind of uncertainty. He could read weather patterns, timber load, snowpack, ice stress. But people—people were different. They shifted. They left holes when they went. They came back in ways that rewrote the ground under his feet.

He finally stepped forward.

"Mind if I sit?" he asked quietly.

She looked up. Her eyes caught the firelight, and something in them softened when she saw him standing there—not guarded, but open in a way that made the air between them feel warmer.

"Please," she said.

He took the chair across from her. For a moment he just sat with his elbows resting loosely on his knees, staring into the fire because it was easier than looking directly at her.

"You're really back," he said after a while, and kept his voice low because anything louder felt like it might break something delicate between them.

"I am," she whispered.

He nodded slowly. It wasn't the return itself that tightened his chest—it was the way she said it, as if the decision had cost her something and given her something all at once.

"How was the drive?" he asked.

"Cold. Quiet." She tucked a foot under her and pulled the blanket up a little higher. "But good. Clearer than the airport."

He huffed a breath that wasn't quite a laugh. "Airport clarity. That's a first."

Her smile warmed the air between them another degree.

She looked down at her mug. "I didn't want to run again. Not from this place. Not from…" She trailed off, voice thinning like a thread pulled too fine.

"Not from yourself," he finished.

She nodded. Her throat worked as she swallowed.

He watched her fingers trace the rim of the mug. The gesture was quiet, but it held a world. Fear. Relief. Hope. Maybe even something he wasn't ready to name yet.

"I'm not very good at leaving things clean," she said softly. "Or coming back without making a mess of it."

He let the words settle before answering. "Storms make messes. People just try to walk through them."

She looked at him then—really looked—and he felt the weight of it in a way that made him sit back slightly, as if the honesty between them had a physical presence.

"I didn't tell you everything," she said. "I mean—I tried. With the letters. But I didn't know how to say it out loud yet."

"I know."

The admission left his mouth before he could second-guess it. He hadn't meant it as forgiveness, and it wasn't an accusation. It was simply true.

A quiet stretched, not uncomfortable, not tense—just full.

He leaned back in his chair, running a hand through his hair, dislodging a bit of sawdust that floated to the floor. He watched it fall, buying himself a moment.

"When you left this morning," he said, "I kept thinking that maybe I'd pushed too hard. Shut down too fast." His voice went rougher at the edges. "That I'd turned into the thing I promised myself I wouldn't be again."

Her brows furrowed. "You didn't—"

"Yeah," he said gently. "I did."

She shook her head, but he didn't let himself get pulled into denial—not from her, not from himself.

"I've done that for years," he continued. "I get blindsided, and I close off. It feels safer than sorting through the pieces." He swallowed. "But it's not safer. Not really. It just... keeps a person alone."

Something flickered across her face—recognition or agreement or something deeper.

"I didn't want to make you feel like you had to hide," he said.

"I didn't mean to hide," she whispered. "I just didn't know how to show up without disappointing someone."

He heard the truth in that, and it loosened something inside him he hadn't realized was clenched.

Silence settled again, but it wasn't sharp or heavy. It had space in it. Breath.

He shifted forward, resting his forearms on his thighs. "You don't have to figure everything out tonight," he said. "But you should know—" His jaw flexed, and he hesitated, searching for the right shape of the words. "I'm glad you turned back. Even if it scared the hell out of me."

Her laugh broke on a breath. "It scared me, too."

"Good," he said, and she blinked, startled. He offered a small, wry smile. "Means we're both awake."

Her eyes warmed, and something in his chest tugged so hard he had to look at the fire again before he could breathe around it.

She drank from her mug, letting the steam hit her face. Her hands had stopped shaking. Her shoulders sat lower now, the tension leaving in small, earnest increments.

"I don't know what happens next," she said again, but the words carried steadiness instead of fear. "I don't want to push anything before it's ready."

He nodded. "Neither do I."

She drew the blanket closer. A few curls fell around her cheek again, and she didn't bother to smooth them back this time.

He watched her for a moment, not shyly, not openly—just honestly. She looked like someone who had weathered a storm inside and out and finally stepped into warmth she trusted to hold.

He knew that feeling too well.

He exhaled slowly. "Tomorrow morning," he said, "after breakfast, I'm checking the south eave again. It's trying to freeze up. Could use a hand."

Her lips curved. "You want free labor."

"I want someone who won't let me fall off a ladder."

She huffed a quiet laugh. "I can do that."

"Good."

They sat in companionable silence for another long stretch. The fire settled to embers. Snow whispered along the porch. Upstairs, a floorboard sighed beneath the shift of old wood.

He didn't want to push. Didn't want to crowd the quiet.

But he also didn't want to end the night without saying one more truth.

"I didn't want to see you leave this morning," he said quietly.

She looked up—truly looked—and her eyes glimmered in the lamplight. "I didn't want to leave."

The admission hit him low in the chest—clean, honest, and warm.

He felt his mouth pull into a small smile he didn't try to hide. "Then I'm glad the storm had opinions."

"Me, too," she whispered.

He stood slowly, giving her time to adjust, but she didn't pull back. He picked up her empty mug and his own, hand brushing hers just briefly.

"Get some sleep," he said, voice softer now. "Tomorrow's long."

She nodded, gaze anchored to his. "Goodnight, Evan."

"Goodnight, Lila."

He watched her climb the stairs, her steps slow and steady. When she reached the landing, she paused, looking back at him with a hint of something—hope, maybe. Or gratitude. Or just the relief of being seen.

Whichever it was, it settled into him like warmth spreading through cold fingers.

When she disappeared down the hall, he finally let out the breath he hadn't realized he'd been holding.

The lodge exhaled with him—wood popping, fire shifting, stairs settling. And for the first time since she'd left that morning, something in him aligned again.

Not fixed.

Not resolved.

But right.

He cleaned the mugs, checked the locks, banked the fire, and made one last slow walk through the quiet halls. When he finally climbed the stairs, he moved more easily, as if the weight he carried wasn't quite so heavy now.

He paused outside her door—not close enough to intrude, just close enough to feel the warmth radiating under it—and let himself believe, just for a moment, that tomorrow might be made of small, steady things they could both hold.

Then he turned toward his room, the soft rhythm of the lodge beneath his feet, and let the storm outside do what storms always did—blow through, quiet, and leave the world a little clearer than before.

Chapter 34

The storm had thinned overnight but never quite stopped. Snow drifted past the windows in a slow, hypnotic fall, soft enough to erase the sharp edges of the world. The fire burned down to a deep bed of coals, painting the room in honeyed light that blurred everything tender.

Lila sat on the rug with her back against the couch, a quilt pulled over her knees and a mug warm in her hands. The air smelled of pine, cinnamon, and a trace of smoke. Juniper purred near her feet, a small gray knot of contentment. The mantel clock ticked softly, matching her pulse.

The house held the kind of peace that comes only after effort—after the day's work had been done, after enough laughter and soup and quiet words had mended what storms had tried to unravel.

Evan sat across from her, one arm hooked over his knee, the firelight catching the gold in his beard. His hands were nicked from ladder work earlier; a faint line of sawdust still clung to his cuff. He looked tired in the good way—steady, at rest.

Neither spoke for a while. The silence between them no longer felt like distance. It felt chosen.

Lila sipped her tea and studied him. "You always sit like that," she said softly.

He blinked. "Like what?"

"With one arm like you're ready to get up, but you never do."

He smiled, faint but real. "Force of habit. I've been ready to leave most places my whole life."

Her heart tugged. "And now?"

His gaze met hers. "Now I don't feel like I have to."

The words landed quietly, but they rippled through her. She smiled. "That's good."

"It is," he said, then looked back at the fire. "You always seem surprised when something's good."

"Maybe I am. I spent too long measuring happiness by how many people were watching. When I finally got quiet, I didn't recognize what peace looked like."

"And now?" he asked.

She drew the quilt closer. "Now it looks like this."

The fire popped, sending a spark skyward before fading. His hand rested near hers on the rug. The distance between their fingers was smaller than it had been that morning.

The pull wasn't heat—it was gravity.

She watched the play of light across his knuckles, the faint tremble in his hand, the steady rise and fall of his chest. The silence wrapped around them like another blanket.

When she finally spoke, her voice was soft. "Evan?"

He looked up. "Hmm?"

"I thought coming here was an accident." She smiled faintly. "Now I think maybe it was something else."

"What?"

"A beginning."

He didn't smile this time. He just looked at her like someone watching the horizon open. "You make it sound like I had a choice in believing in you."

"You didn't," she whispered.

He moved closer, unhurried. She didn't pull back. Their knees brushed under the quilt—warmth rising between them, not urgent, just sure. His hand lifted, slow and careful, and brushed her cheek. Callused fingers met soft skin. She closed her eyes at the tenderness of it.

"You're warm," he said.

"You're cold," she answered, smiling.

He laughed, quiet as breath. His thumb traced the line of her jaw, memorizing.

Lila's heart swelled—not the rush of newness, but recognition. She opened her eyes. He was watching her, steady and present.

He leaned in, their foreheads touching first. She felt his breath, smelled pine and melting snow. The pause between them was reverence.

When he kissed her, it was soft, the bare meeting of lips and the hush of everything else falling away. It felt like a promise written in a language older than words. Her heart fluttered in her chest as a warmth spread to her that had nothing to do with the fire that popped again.

They smiled against each other. When they finally parted, neither moved far.

She rested her head against his shoulder. His arm came around her, easy and certain.

Outside, snow kept falling—quiet, unhurried, patient.

"Evan?" she murmured.

"Mm?"

"I'm not going anywhere."

He rested his chin against her hair. "Good," he said. "Neither am I."

They stayed that way, the world narrowed to the rhythm of breathing and the soft glow of firelight.

Chapter 35

Evan worked by the woodpile that afternoon, splitting what was left of last season's logs. The air carried that late-winter brightness—sharp but forgiving—and every breath came with the scent of pine and meltwater. The rhythm of the axe steadied him. Lift. Swing. Split. The sound echoed across the clearing and left nothing behind but truth.

He wanted this life.

The wanting surprised him less than it should have. For years, he'd told himself the lodge was enough. That quiet was meant to be maintained, not shared. That wanting more was how things broke.

Lila had undone that belief without ever arguing with it.

She hadn't arrived demanding space or certainty. She'd simply stepped into the quiet and treated it like something alive. Something worth listening to. She brought warmth without taking anything from him. She paid attention. She stayed.

He set another log on the stump and brought the axe down hard. The split was clean, final. He liked work that behaved that way. Effort in. Clarity out.

When the last log was stacked, he leaned on the handle and looked toward the lake. The snow shimmered in the afternoon light, the ice thinning into narrow, glinting ribbons near the shore. Beyond the trees, the old cabin stood in soft silhouette.

For years, it had lived in the back of his mind as a project he never started. Not forgotten. Just postponed. A structure without intention.

Now it felt different.

He saw it the way she had—windows open, light on the floor, the kind of space that didn't exist to impress anyone. A place built slowly. A place meant to hold people, not pass them through.

It struck him then how easily the word we had come to him when he'd asked her to help. No hesitation. No fear. Just truth.

For the first time, the idea of a shared future didn't feel like surrender.

It felt like steadiness.

He wiped his forehead with the back of his hand and smiled at nothing.

Footsteps crunched behind him.

She came down the path with her wool cap pulled low and her cheeks flushed from the cold. The sight of her still caught him off guard—not because she didn't belong here, but because she did. Effortlessly. Like the place had been waiting.

"You've been out here for hours," she called.

He grinned. "Long enough to remember I'm bad at stopping."

"That tracks," she said. "Ruth warned me."

"She would."

She stepped closer, brushing sawdust from her sleeve. "Everyone here knows you."

He leaned the axe against the pile. "And you?"

"Not yet," she said, tugging her gloves tighter. "But I'm learning."

The words landed deeper than he expected. He watched her a moment longer than necessary, taking in the quiet confidence she carried now. The way she stood like she didn't need to perform her presence.

"Evan?" she said softly.

He shook his head once. "Just thinking."

"That sounds dangerous."

"Not today," he said. "Today it's honest."

She waited.

"I used to think the lodge was the end of the line," he said. "That I'd built what I was meant to build and that wanting anything else meant I was ungrateful." He met her gaze. "You reminded me that building something and living inside it aren't the same thing."

Her thumb brushed his knuckles, tentative but sure. "Maybe they don't have to be separate anymore."

He nodded. "I don't think they do."

She took his hand without hesitation. Her fingers were cold, but the warmth followed quickly, settling in his chest like something that had been waiting there a long time.

They stood like that while the snow softened underfoot and winter loosened its grip around them. He didn't rush the moment. Didn't name it. It didn't need a name yet.

When she leaned her head against his shoulder, he rested his cheek against her hat and closed his eyes. The cold touched his face. Her warmth balanced it.

"I used to think silence was what I wanted most," he murmured.

"And now?" she asked.

"Now I know better," he said. "Quiet's only good when it's shared."

Her laughter was soft, unguarded. It fit.

They stayed until the light thinned and the first stars showed through the pale sky. Behind them, the lodge lights flicked on, steady and familiar.

Evan squeezed her hand once before they turned back, their steps falling into the same rhythm without effort.

The world around them was wide and still.

For the first time, his heart was not echoing inside it.

It was full—of her, of this place, and of what came next.

Chapter 36

D ays passed quietly after the storm, the kind of days that slipped between hours instead of counting them. The roads stayed passable, the sky a patient gray that never quite cleared. The lodge fell back into its steady rhythm: guests trickled in and out, Ruth's baking perfumed the air, and the woodstove in the lobby gave its loyal crackle.

Lila had fallen into that rhythm, too. Morning coffee with Ruth before the sun burned through the fog. Afternoons spent walking the trail behind the lodge or helping Evan patch something that didn't strictly need fixing. She still caught herself waiting for the next departure—hers, someone's—but the thought no longer brought restlessness. It brought calm.

She'd stopped checking her phone days ago. It sat on the nightstand, half-buried beneath a folded scarf. Her inbox could wait. The world could wait.

Today, Evan had asked her to wear boots she didn't mind getting dirty. That was all he'd said before disappearing outside after breakfast, bundled in his coat and quiet purpose. He'd left the kind of mystery that made her smile.

Now she followed him along a path that wound past the back edge of the property, where the lake curved out of view and the trees thickened. The snow here was deeper, unbroken except for his footprints. The air smelled sharper, more like pine and the faint promise of thaw.

She tugged her hat down against the wind. "You're sure this isn't a trap to make me haul firewood?"

He glanced over his shoulder, smiling. "I'm saving that job for tomorrow."

"Good. I'll schedule my nap accordingly."

They walked another few minutes in easy silence. He carried a set of keys in his pocket that jingled with each step. The sound was comforting.

Finally, they reached a small clearing she didn't remember seeing before. A single cabin sat at its center, half-sunken in snow, its porch sagging at one corner. Time and weather had worn the paint to a ghost of its former color, but the bones of it were strong—square windows, a stone chimney, a roofline that seemed to bow politely toward the lake.

Lila slowed, taking it in. "It's beautiful," she said. "In a broken sort of way."

Evan smiled faintly. "That's one way to put it."

He climbed the porch steps, each one creaking beneath his boots. "This used to be one of the original guest cabins.

Built before the lodge, back when the place was still a fishing camp. It's been empty for years."

She followed him to the door, brushing snow from the railing. "Why hasn't anyone fixed it?"

"Because fixing things takes time," he said, unlocking the door. "And sometimes time's the hardest thing to find."

The hinges groaned as he pushed it open. Cold air spilled out, tinged with cedar and dust. Inside, the cabin was simple: one large room with a small fireplace, a window seat overlooking the lake, and a loft under the eaves. The floors were scarred but solid. A beam near the ceiling carried initials carved by someone decades ago.

Lila stepped inside and turned slowly, seeing past the cobwebs and age. "You could do a lot with this."

"That's what I was thinking," he said quietly.

He walked to the window, brushed frost from the glass, and looked out at the lake. "I've been meaning to do something with this place for years. But it's not a guest cabin anymore, not really. The lodge is enough for that." He turned back to her, his expression thoughtful but certain. "I want it to be something different. Something new."

She tilted her head. "Like what?"

He hesitated for a breath, as if weighing how much of the thought to speak aloud. "You remember the night we talked about quiet—how it isn't so bad with someone to share it?"

"I remember," she said softly.

He nodded. "I've been thinking about that. About how people come here to escape, but maybe what they're really looking for is space to hear themselves again. You've seen it—writers, painters, people burnt out. This town helps them breathe."

Lila's chest tightened in a way that felt good. "It helped me." She knew, with a clarity that surprised her, that she would never again hand her voice over to keep the noise down.

He smiled. "Then maybe it can help others, too." He gestured around them. "I thought we could turn this into a retreat cabin. A place where people can come to create. To be still. To find the quiet."

Her eyes widened. "We?"

"Yeah," he said simply. "I can handle the repairs. You've got the vision. You see things differently. I'd like to do this with you."

For a moment, she couldn't speak. The words had come without flourish or pretense, but they hit her harder than any grand gesture could have.

She looked around the small cabin again—the rough wood, the smell of dust and cold air, the possibility lingering in every shadow. She could already picture it: walls sanded smooth, a work table near the window, shelves filled with sketchbooks and mugs. Maybe a small record player. Maybe a cat that refused to leave.

"You're serious," she said finally.

Evan's smile reached his eyes this time. "Completely."

She let out a laugh, shaking her head. "You're asking a travel blogger who quit her job to help build a creative retreat. That's either poetic or foolish."

"Both," he said. "But the good kind."

Her heart swelled. "What made you think of this?"

He shrugged, glancing around. "You. This place needed a reason to wake up again. So did I."

The honesty of it caught her off guard. She crossed the small room and stood beside him, looking out the window. The lake stretched beneath a pale sky, half-frozen and shining faintly where the wind brushed the surface clear.

"I think it's perfect," she said.

"Even like this?" he asked, glancing at the cracked plaster and the layer of dust on the sill.

"Especially like this," she said. "It's waiting for someone to see what it can be."

He looked at her then—really looked—and the warmth in his eyes was like an invitation. "That's what you do, isn't it? You see potential in things most people overlook."

"And you fix things people think can't be fixed."

"Maybe that's why this makes sense," he said.

The quiet stretched again, not awkward, just full. Lila felt it move through her, as real as the sunlight creeping across the floorboards.

"Let's do it," she said.

He turned to her, eyebrows lifting. "You mean it?"

"I do." She smiled, feeling the words settle in her chest like an anchor and a promise all at once. "Let's make this our project. Something built from the quiet instead of in spite of it."

He nodded slowly, almost reverently, then reached for her hand. His palm was rough and warm against hers. "We'll start when the thaw comes," he said. "It'll give us time to plan."

"Plan," she repeated, smiling at the word as if it were new.

They stood there a while longer, side by side, looking out at the snow and the lake beyond it. The wind slipped through the cracked window frame, and she leaned closer, instinctively, the way she always did now. His arm brushed hers, a small reminder that they were no longer strangers trying to protect themselves from the cold.

This small cabin, this fragile plan, this unspoken promise wasn't a grand declaration. It was something simpler. A future built not on ownership but on belonging.

As they stepped back onto the porch, the sky opened just enough for light to break through, catching the ice on the trees and scattering it like glass. Evan turned the key in the old lock, then slipped it into her hand instead of his pocket.

"For safekeeping," he said. What he was offering wasn't safe. It was unfinished, exposed, and dependent on someone else staying. And he chose it anyway.

She looked down at it—tarnished brass, edges worn smooth from years of use. "You trust me with this?"

"I do," he said, quiet but sure.

Her breath caught, the cold and warmth tangling in her chest. She closed her hand around the key. "Then I guess it's settled."

He grinned. "Welcome to your first renovation."

She laughed and shook her head. "You say that like you don't know what you're getting into."

"Oh, I do," he said, eyes bright with something more than amusement. "And that's exactly why I'm asking."

They started back toward the lodge, boots sinking into the soft snow, the wind whispering through the trees. Behind them, the little cabin waited—still, hopeful, and ready to be something new.

Lila glanced back once and felt a quiet certainty rise through her like warmth from the fire they'd shared days before.

It wasn't about escaping anymore. It was about building.

And this time, she wouldn't be doing it alone.

Chapter 37

The Midwinter Festival always came on the first clear night after the long storm, when the snow had settled and the air felt like glass. Strings of lights crossed Winter Market Square from tree to post to storefront, warm gold against the blue edge of evening. Frost clung to the bunting on the bakery stall. Pine, cider, and wood smoke folded into the cold until the scent felt thick enough to taste.

Lila stood near the edge of the crowd with her camera strap across her chest, breath lifting in soft clouds. A waltz drifted from the bandstand where Nora's cousin played a violin too delicate for the weather. Children hurried past with cocoa, scarves trailing behind them. Near the ice-carving table, curls shaved from a lantern-shaped block skittered away like glass petals.

She lifted the camera. The lens fogged, cleared, then found the small, true things.

A girl pressing her gloves to a violin case for warmth.

Ruth leaning over a tray of cookies while Walter pretended not to steal one.

A boy balancing on a snowbank, his mother's hand hovering just out of frame.

A couple laughing at nothing anyone else could see.

The shutter kept time with her pulse. She wasn't chasing perfection or approval. She was letting the night be what it already was.

Near the bonfire, Evan talked with Bennie from the hardware store, both of them flushed from heat and cold. When he looked up and found her, the smile he gave was small and private.

I see you.

She lowered the camera and let the moment pass without capturing it.

"City girl," Ruth said at her elbow, pressing a cup into her hands. "You've hidden behind that thing all night."

"Occupational hazard," Lila said, fingers stinging as hot cider met cold air.

"Still writing?" Ruth asked.

"Maybe," Lila said. "Just not the way I used to."

"Good," Ruth said, already moving on, calling something about marshmallows that made Walter groan.

The music slowed. Couples turned near the fire. Snow whispered under boots. Someone rang the raffle bell and a cheer rose. Lila took one more photograph—Evan laughing, firelight caught in his eyes—then lowered the camera and didn't lift it again.

He crossed to her through the crowd.

"You found the best light," he said.

"It found me."

They stood shoulder to shoulder, close enough to feel heat on their faces and cold at their backs.

"You working," he asked, "or staying for the good part?"

"Both," she said. "Mostly staying."

He nodded, easy and certain. "Then it's a success."

She could have told him about the frame she missed—the cookie dropped, the friends who split theirs without comment—but some things felt better left unshared. They watched the square breathe. A fiddle string lifted and settled. Someone sang just off the beat and made it better.

It struck her how far she had come, not in miles but in meaning. Months ago, she would have taken these images for proof. Tonight, she took them to remember. This was what belonging looked like when no one asked her to perform.

Later, in her room, she uploaded the photos and let them fill the screen. Firelit faces. Hands meeting. Laughter mid-breath. None of it perfect. All of it true.

She opened her blog window. The cursor blinked, waiting.

The Warmest Place I Know

It is not a city or a mountain or a map point.

It is where silence hums instead of echoes.

Where kindness moves slower than talk but reaches farther.

Where the fire burns steadily and no one asks what you lost—

only if you are cold.
Tonight I stood under lights in a town called Midwinter.
I didn't need to perform.
I didn't need to be anyone else.
I only needed to belong.
I think I do.

She read it once. Then typed two words at the bottom.

Anonymous entry.

She hit publish without checking a count.

At the window, the square still glowed below, the last song carrying up the hill. She lifted a hand without thinking. Down by the bonfire, Evan looked toward the lodge at the same moment and tipped his chin.

It felt like an answer.

For the first time in years, she wasn't watching her life from the outside.

She was in it.

Chapter 38

Morning poured through the lodge windows in wide stripes of honeyed light. The storm had spent itself and left the world sharp and clean. Coffee drifted from the kitchen, threaded with wood smoke and a hint of maple.

Evan flipped a pancake and smiled when it landed right.

Lila sat on the counter with her hair still a little wild from sleep, scrolling her phone without urgency. She wasn't reading headlines. She was finishing something.

"You're supposed to wait until they're all done," Evan said.

"I am waiting," she said, reaching for one anyway. "I'm just... adjacent to the process."

Juniper perched on a chair, tail ticking like a metronome.

"You're teaching her bad habits," Evan told the cat.

"She came preloaded," Lila said. "You just didn't notice."

His laugh came easy now, low and unguarded. It still surprised her how much she liked the sound of it. How little it asked of her in return.

They carried breakfast to the hearth, where yesterday's fire had gone soft to ash. Evan knelt and stacked kindling with the same care he brought to anything that mattered.

"Here," he said, handing her a split piece of pine. "Fire doesn't start with force. It starts with space."

"You're romanticizing it," she said, though her smile gave her away.

"Rush it and it smothers. Give it air and it takes."

They leaned in as the match flared. The flame caught, small and steady, then settled into itself. It grew because they let it.

Lila set her phone facedown on the rug.

"I posted something this morning," she said.

Evan didn't look up. He didn't tense. He just waited.

"I didn't explain everything," she continued. "I didn't argue. I just said the truth. That I blurred lines I shouldn't have. That I let speed matter more than integrity. That I'm stepping back from anything that isn't fully mine."

He nodded once. "That sounds like you."

"I also shut down the contracts that were waiting for me to come back loud and busy and apologetic," she said. "No sponsored trips. No automated voice. No chasing reach just to prove I still exist."

The fire settled into a low, confident burn.

"I'm going to write slower," she said. "Long-form. Essays. Maybe anonymously for a while. Maybe not at all, some weeks. And when I do use tools, I'll say so. No pretending." She exhaled. "I don't need to win anyone back. I just need to stand where I can see myself."

"That's a good place to stand," he said.

She hesitated, then smiled to herself. "I also saw something last night. Someone posted a response under one of the threads."

His hands stilled, just briefly.

"Nothing flashy," she said. "No grand defense. Just... context. A reminder that people are allowed to change their process when they realize something isn't right. That character shows up in what someone does next, not in how loud they are when they're cornered."

He cleared his throat. "People say things."

"Yes," she said gently. "But this one sounded like someone who fixes broken steps without signing his name."

He winced. "You didn't need to notice that."

"I know," she said. "And I'm not going to mention it again. You'd hate that." She bumped her shoulder into his. "But I noticed."

The moment passed without ceremony. That felt right, too.

They ate on the rug with their backs against the couch while Juniper claimed the warmest patch by the hearth. Outside, snow glittered in the sun. Inside, the sounds were ordinary and perfect—coffee cooling too fast, syrup on fingers, the soft crackle of flame finding its rhythm.

Evan watched her watch the fire. His chest felt full, not because the world was quiet, but because it wasn't empty anymore.

"Think the retreat cabin needs a fireplace like this?" she asked.

"Definitely," he said. "Every good beginning does."

She rested her head on his shoulder. Neither of them moved. The fire breathed slow and sure.

"Maybe the quiet was always good," she said.

"Maybe," he said. "We just needed the right company."

They sat there as the morning climbed the walls and Midwinter stirred awake below—doors opening, boots on snow, the promise of work and warmth and days that would keep coming.

Things still needed tending.

But nothing needed fixing.

Nothing needed proving.

They had built something that knew how to hold.

The Quiet Hours

Excerpt

Chapter 1

Nora West unlocked the Blue Finch while the sky was still undecided. Not night anymore, not quite morning. Just that narrow band of blue where the world felt held in place, waiting to be told what came next.

She liked opening before sunrise. The café belonged to her most in these hours, before footsteps and opinions and the low murmur of expectation. Before anyone needed anything from her and she could enjoy the quiet of her kitchen.

Inside, the air was warm and faintly sweet, yesterday's bread and clean wood layered together. She flicked on the front lights, then the ones over the counter, each switch clicked in the same order every morning. Habit wasn't laziness. It was insurance. If she did things the same way, the day usually followed suit.

Coat off. Scarf on the hook. Apron folded and waiting.

She crossed to the ovens and turned them on, the familiar clicks answering back. Heat first. Always. She checked the thermometer, then the trays of dough resting under cloths on the prep table, before glancing at the soup warmer near the back counter to make sure the pilot light had held overnight.

With one finger, she pressed into a loaf hard enough to leave a shallow indent, then watched the slow return.

Ready meant different things to different people. To her, it meant steady. Predictable. No surprises.

The espresso machine came next, followed by the drip pots she kept cycling through the morning rush. Water filled, switch flipped, the low warming sound settling into the room. That sound had carried her through more mornings than she could count. She liked the feeling of being prepared for what the day had in store for her. She liked knowing what was coming.

She wiped the counters, even though she had wiped them before locking up the night prior. The cloth moved in straight lines. Corners first. Edges last. Flour dusted the back of her hand from a bowl she hadn't fully covered, and she left it there longer than necessary, a small reminder that perfection wasn't required to begin.

Then she filled a to-go cup with coffee, two sugars, and a splash of cream. From the fridge, she pulled a breakfast roll and a foil-wrapped egg sandwich she'd assembled the night before, sliding both into the oven. By the time it was warmed, the front door opened.

Nora didn't look up. She didn't have to.

She slid his breakfast roll into a bag and set it beside his coffee on the counter. Feeding people had always felt easier than talking to them.

Mason Pike liked to stop in before opening, grab what he needed, and get to his job sites early. She liked knowing he was fed before the day asked too much of him. She'd known the man for years. He'd live off fast food and microwaved burritos if she hadn't convinced him to start swinging by the café at least for breakfast.

He took the cup. "You're spoiling me."

She smiled faintly. "You're here before dawn. That earns provisions."

He took a sip, then another, eyes half-closing for a second in appreciation. "Worth getting up for."

Snow clung to the shoulders of his coat, melting into the wool. As he looked around, his gaze drifted automatically to the ceiling light above the pastry case. It buzzed faintly, uneven.

"How long has that been going on?" he asked.

"Started yesterday afternoon."

He nodded once, set his coffee down, and reached up without another word. She watched him work, the practiced ease of his movements, the way he didn't rush but didn't waste time either.

"Still working with Evan on that cabin at Ember Lodge?" she asked, casual, the way she always kept it.

He huffed softly. "Sadly. Seems like a never-ending project."

She smiled to herself. "I thought winter was supposed to slow things down."

"It does," he said, tightening the bulb. "Just not there. Old buildings don't believe in rest."

Something clicked into place behind the fixture. The light steadied.

He moved to the back door next, fingers testing the hinge before she could mention it. The metal scraped softly as he adjusted it, easing the drag the cold always brought.

"How's it holding up?" she asked.

"Stubborn," he said. "But honest."

She liked that about him. That he noticed. That he paid attention to the small issues before they became real problems. That he didn't wait to be asked.

"Thanks," she said, because even familiarity deserved acknowledgment.

He picked up his coffee again and gave her a brief, easy smile. "I'll swing by later with the lumber list."

"Okay."

He slid some cash onto the counter, took the bag, and was gone as quietly as he'd arrived.

Nora stood still for a moment after he left, listening. Ovens warming. Espresso machine humming. No voices. No rush.

This was the part of the day she trusted. The hours before the quiet turned into chaos. Before the lunch crowd arrived. Before decisions multiplied.

She moved to the computer at the end of the counter and logged in, expecting the usual. Supply confirmations. A reminder from the book club. Someone asking if they could reserve the small room saved for larger groups of visitors.

The email from the Winter Market committee sat at the top of her inbox.

She opened it without sitting down.

They thanked her for agreeing to participate again. Noted the increased interest in her stall last year. Mentioned demand. Growth. Opportunity.

They asked her to confirm the expanded footprint they'd suggested weeks ago. Double frontage. Additional prep space. More product visibility.

She didn't reread it. Didn't tally hours or imagine crowds. Didn't picture the café empty while she stood behind a bigger table, smiling until her cheeks ached.

She typed yes.

Short. Clean. Sent.

The sound of the email leaving felt louder than it should have in the quiet room.

She poured herself coffee and leaned against the counter, wrapping both hands around the mug. The heat pressed into her palms, grounding. Outside, the sky lightened, the mountains outside of Midwinter beginning to separate themselves from the dark.

She watched Mason's truck pull away through the front window, tires crunching softly over snow. When the sound faded, the café felt suddenly larger.

Too large.

She returned to the computer and opened the email again. This time she read every line. The logistics. The expectations. The polite certainty that she could handle it.

Her chest tightened, not sharply. Slowly. Like something heavy settling where calm usually lived.

More space meant more product. More demands on her. More eyes.

She looked around the Blue Finch. Chairs stacked neatly. Pastry case waiting. The quiet she had built her life around, brick by brick, morning by morning.

The ovens chimed, ready.

Nora stood alone behind the counter, coffee cooling in her hands, and realized she had agreed to something she was not emotionally ready to hold.

Also by Haven

Cloverton Romance Series

(with Marci Wilson)
Turn the Page: Book One
Faked With Love: Book Two
Music of the Heart: Book Three
In Full Bloom: Book Four
Tattered Dreams: Book Five
By Design: Book Six
A Cloverton Christmas (short story)
The Perfect Blend: Book Seven
A Healing Touch: Book Eight
Against the Grain: Book Nine
Written in Stone: Book Ten
The Innkeeper's Christmas (short story)